LOADED FOR BEAR

Lee heard a grunt, turned and saw a grizzly bear—a big bear the color of cinnamon. It was up on its hinds not forty feet away, its paws folded to its chest, and was looking at him, weaving its head slowly from side to side.

The Indian girl shouted, and Lee knew what she would do next. He turned just as she was hauling her brand new Winchester repeater out of its scabbard at the paint's shoulder.

We'll get out of this, Lee thought, if that squaw doesn't start shooting. Might as well send Surrey a telegraph message as start firing rifle shots in these mountains!

He gestured "No," and finally shouted, "No shooting, God damnit!"

The bear didn't care for that shouting—likely had been out on the mountain hunting marmots for his winter sleep. Didn't like the shouting at all.

Lee heard the bear squeal—exactly the sound a huge pig might have made—turned, and saw the animal drop suddenly to all fours, almost out of sight in the dwarf pines, and come for him. It looked like a great gold-brown rug, suddenly animated and given the power to charge, fronted with a gaping, wrinkled black muzzle packed with yellow teeth. . . .

BUCKSKIN #9

CROSSFIRE
COUNTRY

Roy LeBeau

LEISURE BOOKS ✿ NEW YORK CITY

A LEISURE BOOK

Published by

Dorchester Publishing Co., Inc.
6 East 39th Street
New York, NY 10016

Printed in the United States of America

CROSSFIRE COUNTRY

Chapter One

In the fall, an old Red-nigger trespassed onto Spade Bit.

Bud Bent, nearly as old as the Indian, saw him riding down from the breaks on a little spotted pony. Bent saw the man was an Indian at more than a half-mile distance; he had the slouching, hump-shouldered way of riding. And when Bent had his Volcanic out of the saddle-bucket, and levered, he was close enough to see the Indian was old, and riding wrapped in a red-stripe Canadian blanket against the cold. Bud looked sharp for other savages—the Redmen were almost done, now, and rotting on reservations, but those few wild bucks still prone to breaking out, drunk and dressed in white man's castoff clothing, were men to beware of.

Bent looked, but the broad sweep of

grassland seared here and there with brown from early-season frosts showed no rider but one. Might be some much higher, trotting the slopes of the Old Man, but Bent doubted it. They'd hardly show their hand by having this old one come fumbling down so near the horse-herds, the Spade Bit hands.

The old Indian was riding as if his ass was sore. Was riding as if all his bones were sore, come to that—and, closer now, Bent saw the old man was worn to a frazzle, his pinched face as seamed and brown as a ragged old pocket wallet. Bent was no Spring chicken himself, however, and had learned long ago that age doesn't necessarily mellow a man. Hadn't, after all, mellowed him.

He kept the Volcanic, cocked, across his saddle-bow, pulled Sally up, and waited for the savage to come on.

It was something to Bent's credit that he rested calm since, as a young boy, he had lost his mother to Blackfeet Indians during a river-stop on the Oregon Trace. The savages, a small bunch led by a war shaman named Bear-eyes, had lifted the woman when she went into the reeds to make water, had taken her away screaming amid gunfire, made a getaway clean, and had, in the next few days, outraged the poor creature, penetrated her with sticks and such, and had, wearying of her, sliced off her breasts and torn her eyes out. She had died then—thankful, no doubt, to go.

8

All this young Bud, his father and brothers had heard of later—after they'd gotten to Oregon, in fact—in the manner in which such tales became current. The revelations of drunken Blackfeet at wintering Forts, fur trades, squaw trades, and camp gossips.

The Bents, thereafter, in amends perhaps at being just too late getting to the river-bank that hot afternoon with their rifles—the Bents, little Bud among them, though too young to blame, became for a while killers of Indians, and Blackfeet in particular, with a vision of Mrs. Bent's exposure and suffering always in their minds. The Bents killed a number of Blackfeet Indians, men, women, and cubs, until the smallpox did their work for them, and better.

Bud Bent was the last to stop Rednigger hunting, but did so finally, wearying of it. Bear-eyes, in any case, had died, drowned crossing the Snake in 1873.

Something to old Bud's credit, therefore or to the credit of those wearying Indians long ago slain that he did not take the casual opportunity to empty the old Indian's saddle without parley.

Times had changed, of course—though not enough to allow a savage to ride across ranch land and not be injured for it if caught—and, after all, the Redman was old. So was Bud Bent. Some fellow feeling there, perhaps, of aching joints in icy weather.

The Indian, who must have seen Bent as soon as or sooner than Bent had seen him, rode slowly up to him and stopped. Bent saw the old man had a shotgun with a busted stock hanging from his saddle-bow on a length of twine. No other arms apparent.

The Indian had a rheumy and wrinkled eye, but sharp enough. He sat his pony, a rack-ribbed pinto, and very small, and gave Bent a considerable and detailed study.

Then, *"Je cherche Mohr-gonne,"* he said, or something like it.

Bent had heard Canuck French before and grunted Indian, too, but he was not the Idaho wrangler to play any talk but plain American.

"If you're askin' for Lee Morgan, then by God say it in English—an' tell me why the hell I should bother."

The old man gave Bent another hard look. If looks could kill, Bent would have at least felt poorly. Then he slowly said, in English plain enough, though it creaked, "I look . . . for . . . Morgan."

"Do you now?" Bent said. "And what for?"

But the old man had done his talking, apparently satisfied that he'd found the right place at any rate, and content enough to wait Bent out . . . to wait 'till his silence brought him to the man he'd come to see.

The thin-lipped mouth, brown and wrinkled, without much in the way of teeth to obstruct it, clamped tight shut. His gaze drifted away from Bud Bent as if the wrangler had turned to campfire smoke, and the old man sat deeper into his rawhide saddle, ready, it seemed, to sit through the winter.

Bud gave a good try at waiting him out.

An hour and more later, some disgruntled, he led the old man, sitting his saddle slouched and seeming asleep, into the Spade Bit timber camp.

Lee Morgan was there—had come up from headquarters two days before to see what was delaying the cut on corral timbers and shed planks and trough boxes. Had come up and snarled some, then had taken his fine fringed buckskin jacket off, rolled up his shirt sleeves, and taken his turn down in the saw-pit.

He was sitting up on a stack of clean cut posts, taking a cup of hot-coal coffee, when Bent and the Red man came riding in. Bud Bent had known Lee Morgan for more than ten years, ever since a quiet kid with a wicked fast revolver-draw had ridden into the mountains to fetch a vengeance on his own father—and that father a legend among the great killers of the west.

That quiet boy had changed considerably.

The blond hair was darker, now—almost brown. The boy's eyes, amber-colored then, had turned darker, too. And harder. Hard as clay-stained granite. The man, a boy no longer, had sized up and filled out. Bigger now than his father had been. And grimly quick with a revolver—the natural fast draw had slicked, smoothed out. Perhaps with not quite the inhuman quickness that had been Buckskin Frank Leslie's gift (and curse) but terribly fast all the same. Terribly fast and with a target-shooter's accuracy at the finish.

"A holy terror in this country, if he chose to be," a sheriff named Berman said about him once, speculating what Lee Morgan might get up to were he not a ranch owner, rich and respectable. And the sheriff had been surely right. But what capabilities, what currents of violence had run in the boy turning man, had been for the most part dammed, suppressed, buried under the endless chores and duties, business and responsibilities that went with high-mountain horse-ranching. Lee Morgan had his anchors buried in the Rocky Mountain pastureland—and, up to two years before, those anchors of duty and labor had kept him a peaceful man, bar some sprees of trouble in San Francisco, some difficulty in the Dakotas.

Up to two years before.

Then, he'd come back from the Dakotas. Rich. Rich on copper shares or some such mining stuff, and happy as a bull buffalo in grassland. Happy for two or three weeks.

The diptheria throat had come to Parker, first, and killed a few kids. Then, in weeks, had moved on down to Grover and struck at the ranches around the small town. Killed another kid or two, an old man named Claude Anstruther, and made some other people sick.

When the disease had run its course in the country, or had seemed to, Lee Morgan's Chinese girl up in Parker had come down with it. At first, she'd rallied fine, and Lee had gone up twice to help her Chinese woman-friend with the nursing. It had not, at first, seemed too serious. S'ien was a strong young woman, no sickly, croupy kid, and she had sand to spare. It had, at first, seemed only some time to spend sick, as most people had to spend, one month or another.

But she got no better. No better at all. Slowly . . . very slowly, the disease began to bring her down, as chasing wolves in deep snow will run and run and weary a stag elk to his end. S'ien got no better. For days, and then weeks, the tissue of corruption stuck in her slender throat, swollen, fiery, leaking its pus and spoiling blood.

After the third week, early one morning, her heart began to labor, to flutter like a wild bird caught in a house, like a bird that's flown in during spring cleaning and can find no open window.

Her friend had sent down-country for Lee to return—and Lee, who raised horses and loved them, rode a fine mare named Sunshine to death, and so rode up from Grover faster than had ever been done.

He'd left the mare dying on Parker's main

street, and run all the way to the far edge of town, to the cottage he'd given his Chinese girl. A slave girl she'd been, years before, when he'd bought her in San Francisco . . .

S'ien was dying.

The diptheria had run and run her. It had wearied her as through deep snow, until she lay worn to the bone, gasping, her black eyes fever bright. The small heart, red and richly brave, that had beat for her through a childhood, a girlhood of horrors . . . that had thudded with her pleasures in Lee's embrace . . . had tapped as sweetly as a drum in the warmth of his protection, his unspoken love, this small, strong heart now failed and failed.

The Chinese girl, her slender throat on fire, lay still, and pale, and dying. She looked up at Lee from her white bed, with eyes as bright with pleasure as fever. Love joined them in that look, as with a rope of gold.

The doctor in Parker then was a man named Pauly, Amos Pauly. A physician from Baltimore, a large, fat, bulky man, and believed to be a good and scientific doctor. It was thought that he had saved several children from the diptheria that might have otherwise died. He had put a silver tube down into their rotting throats, pushed it deep into the mass, then had himself sucked the matter out, spitting it away in a basin. Had done this until the scraps of membrane, the lumps of pus were cleared way. Then had had the child held gasping, trying to scream, upside down by its feet, while with an India rubber bulb, Doctor Pauly had squirted high-proofed spirits of whiskey up into their raw and bleeding throats.

The children had screamed then right enough, and some said that Pauly had killed Michael Patterson's little girl with that treatment. And so he might have, but he saved six others, and in a manner that no one else cared to attempt.

It was this man that Lee Morgan came for that evening, Morgan cursing himself for ever going back down to the Bit at all while S'ien was sick. Morgan came onto the Paulys' front porch, struck hard at the door, and told Pauly to get his gear and come damn quick.

Pauly now was a tired man and just roused from his dinner. And he was a Southerner as well, born and bred. He came to the door, heard Lee out, and told him civilly enough and to his face that he treated no coloreds, and no yellow people either. He suggested that the girl might do better doctored by her own people in the town.

From what Mrs. Pauly later said—and it was generally, and with good reason, believed—Lee Morgan changed right then from a reasonable man, though occasionally violent, to a person of an altogether diffrent sort.

"Doctor," Mrs. Pauly said he said, "if you don't go get your things and medicines and come with me right now as hard as you can, I am going to kill every human person in your house. I will blow out their brains over your dinner table.''

This said in a voice as light and easy as a preacher's at a wedding.

Mrs. Pauly had crouched silent as a rabbit, and as still, in her dining room doorway, as if by being so still and silent she might prevent Morgan from walking into the room from the entrance hall, having killed her husband, to stand easy while firing his heavy revolver at her children, Jake and little Ivy, who sat in their chairs (Ivy's a high-chair that Mister Ferguson had made special for the Paulys after the doctor had set his leg) who sat in their chairs white in the face, waiting for that man to do what he'd just said he would do.

Doctor Pauly was a man grown and no coward. But he was no fool, either.

''Very well,'' he said. ''Upon that threat, I must come.'' He gave Lee the look a man might give some poisonous mindless creature, then turned and went to get his medicines.

All that night, the doctor labored over the dying girl, and did not, for hate, hold back any skill. Lee Morgan and his revolver faded to inconsequence in that night-long struggle between Doctor Pauly and the diptheria.

He very nearly saved her.

It was thought, in fact, that he *had* saved her, when morning came. But just as the sun came full up, while Lee bent over her, whispering something to her, the girl's small heart stuttered suddenly and stopped.

Doctor Pauly left the house soon after that —and was likely glad enough to get out, though Morgan had not, apparently, threatened him or his family again. The Chinese woman, a woman named Ma Ling, left with the doctor. Left Lee Morgan alone with his dead girl.

It may have been this incident—shame, or anger over it—it may have been something else altogether, but Amos Pauly moved away from Parker not two months after, he and his family, bag and baggage. It was known that Morgan sent a wrangler to the doctor's house with a bank draft for one thousand dollars just three days after the girl's death. An apology, that great sum must have been.

The doctor tore the draft to bits in front of the wrangler that brought it, then closed the door in his face. Two months later, Amos Pauly was gone from Parker, and never returned. It left the town a good doctor short, since the only other physician was George Fipps, and he was not well thought of.

Lee Morgan left Parker the same day the girl died; he left the town in a rented buckboard. In the back of that rig, wrapped in silk clothes, and lying buried in a glittering drift of ice out of Swenson's ice-house, lay the girl, S'ien.

That was an odd enough thing to hear about, and Parker was a long-nosed town, but no one came out to see it as Lee Morgan tooled the buckboard down a deserted Main Street, and out onto the southern road. A sight to hear about, but felt unwise to view except from behind curtains, or shop shutters.

Early on the next morning, having driven all night, Lee Morgan returned to Spade Bit with his dead girl. He returned a different man than he had been riding out.

He tooled the buckboard up into the pine grove above the headquarters house, took the girl from her shroud of melting ice, and laid her out in her soaked silks on the soft, rich pine straw of the grove. Left her there in tree shadows while he went back down the slope for a pick and shovel, two wool blankets, Catherine Dowd's silver-backed set of comb and brush, a small sheath knife that McCorkle had made from a hoof-rasp (which sharpened into wicked edges), a package, which he made up himself, of sliced cold elk, that morning's biscuits, and a jar of blackberry preserves Mrs. Summers had brought over weeks before.

He carried these things back up to the grave, and then commenced to dig. No man on the Bit went near him. Sid Sefton had seen Lee driving in, saw him rattling up the track at sunrise. Had seen the shadow of the girl under the drift of ice.

Morgan had said nothing to Sid, but drove

on, and, later that morning, dug the girl's grave just the other side of his father's. Near side, Catherine Dowd was buried.

When the grave was dug, Morgan had come down again, gone to the corrals, and roped out a little spotted mare called Dandy. He filled a two-quart canteen with fresh water, tacked the mare out, slung the canteen cord on the saddle horn, and led the horse away, up into the grove.

Men down at headquarters heard a shot some time later from up in the pines, and one of the men, a new hand called Spots (from his array of freckles) was curious enough to go up the next day to see what was what. He found the girl's narrow grave, and, at her feet, the bigger burial of the mare—thought that considerable quaint (he was a merry, joking man) and would have mentioned it for fun had Bud Bent and the others not warned him.

From that day, Lee Morgan tended to be a solemn man. He would still laugh but the laugh was shorter, usually, than it would have been. He was harder in his dealings with other men, and his look weighed upon them and bore them down, as if by that he said: Who are you . . . that I should take much notice of you?

Men, always somewhat wary of him for his reputation, became still more uneasy with him, as if he threatened them just standing, looking at them.

Still, in the ways of his work, nothing much changed. If anything, he worked harder and drove the men harder. There were stories of the hoof-and-mouth sickness coming north out of Mexico, and he organized the ranchers and horse-people around Grover to patrol against that, to ban buying of that sort of southern stock, to swear to cull their herds of any sickly beasts.

This, and the daily work from an hour before sun-rise, to five hours after dark, chousing, berating, timber cutting, hay binding, nursing cankers, blow-flies, breaks, strains, glanders, splints, bird-ear, thrush. Hunting high-country wolves, low-country coyotes and occasional rustlers and thieves. These last, very unlucky men.

This work, and moving, breeding, marketing, grain-feeding, maintaining gear and buildings, and ordering and paying from six to a dozen violent and cranky men (the number varying with the season) appeared sufficient to smother whatever fire burned in Lee Morgan over the girl's death. The work— and the unlucky horse-thieves were sufficient, up to almost a year after S'ien died.

There was a man named Huffman, a miller and feed merchant who had a place on the Big Chicken, well south of the Old Man. This Huffman was a decent respectable sort of a man, thin, scanty-haired, and not tall. He had an illness of fits, however, which may or may not have been the cause of his bad temper.

He had an ungovernable temper which, though it struck him infrequently, was dangerous enough for people to beware of him.

Huffman had killed a man named Roger Parks after a discussion—not really a quarrel—over a price on feed. They had had their disagreement, and nothing much to that, and Parks had walked out of the mill and over to his wagon. Without calling out, or saying a word, Huffman had suddenly rushed out of the mill building, out along the loading dock, and come up behind Parks with a small revolver in his hand. He had shot Roger Parks in the back without warning, and, when Parks fell, bent down to shoot him again in the side of the head; Parks' wife, Betsy, sitting screaming on the wagon seat during this murder.

It was a measure of Huffman's standing in the community, (he had been a selectman at Grover two years running) and a measure as well of the long record of his being law-abiding and a respectable citizen, that he was not taken out and hanged forthwith for this killing, which was a murder and no mistake.

But Huffman was not hanged and, after some in-and-out at the County court, was not even tried over the affair, it being alleged that his illness fits were likely responsible for that violence.

This judgment, of course, left open the possibility of those brain fits causing further danger to anyone who crossed Mister Huffman, and as a result he was treated gently by the mill and feed customers, and even by his friends and family.

Huffman's temper remained uncertain, but for many months after the Parks shooting, the miller did not try to kill anyone else.

Then, one Tuesday morning, Lee Morgan went to the Big Chicken mill with Charley Potts driving wagon, to pick up an order of twenty sacks of fine-ground wheat grain.

Huffman had only ten sacks, the full order not having been freighted down from the Parker spur, and he and Lee stood at his office door and talked about that, Lee regretting a wasted trip and time off work.

Two men, customers, were standing near Lee and Huffman and later swore that not a single angry word passed between them, though Lee was heard to say he wished Huffman had sent some notice that the grain had not arrived. When he said that though, the two men thought that Huffman did not appear to take it amiss.

Lee Morgan and Huffman had their talk, Lee deciding to take a half load back, as better than none, and walking out onto the dock to help Charlie Potts with the loading.

As he left the building, the two men heard Huffman call after him, saying, "I see that you blame me for this . . . !"

Morgan said nothing but went on to where Charlie Potts was already hauling grain sacks and stacking them down in the wagon.

Huffman then went to the door of the building, and called out, "I take no blame for any matter!"

Morgan turned and looked at him but said nothing.

The two men in the building then saw Huffman come back inside, looking odd— "Looked like he was half-asleep . . ." He walked into his office, fumbled at his workdesk, and then, with a small nickel-plated revolver in his hand, went back outside.

Charlie Potts saw Huffman across the dock, saw the pistol in his hand and shouted, "*Lee!*"

As Lee turned, Huffman called out to him, "No man gives me the lie!" and stepped out onto the dock planking raising the small revolver to fire.

Lee Morgan drew and shot Mister Huffman center and low, through his guts.

Huffman's small revolver went off as he fell back, the bullet shining away through the summer trees, and Huffman sat down hard on the dock planking, his white shirt already red above his buckle. "Why . . . you've shot me!" he said, like a child awakening, and looked up at Lee as if expecting some explanation.

Lee Morgan's face was still as dark water in a rain barrel. He cocked his piece again, and firing off-hand, without appearing to take an aim, he let off a second shot that struck Huffman through his jaw and blew the bone at the side of his head away.

A man named Sundersen was sitting his wagon alongside that edge of the dock at the timee, and later swore that he could see near through Huffman's ruined head—the ear-hole, revealed and pouring blood, seeming to funnel into Huffman's spoiled brain deep enough to come out the other side.

So Sundersen later said, but others said he bent and vomited off his wagon seat and could have seen no such detail.

Then, with revolver-smoke still eddying in the dusty air, Lee had reholstered his Bisley Colt's and stooped to continue loading his horse-grain.

"Jumpin' Jesus," Charlie Potts had said. *"Jumpin' Jesus!"* And he bent again to help him.

This was the Lee Morgan, different and darker than he had been, to whom Bud Bent led the old Indian up at the Spade Bit timber camp.

Morgan, sitting up on a pile of cut rough planks, glanced at them as they rode in, then looked away to say something to a hand named Bob Pete, then to take another drink of his coffee. His flannel shirt was sweated black from buck-sawing.

Bud Bent rode up to him, the old Indian slouching along behind on his rackety paint, and said, "Here's a nigger wants a word with you, Lee. Won't tell me what the fuck it's all about.''

"Won't, huh?" Morgan said, and tossed his cup dregs aside and handed the cup to Bob Pete. Then he turned a little as he sat, and laid his still, heavy gaze on the old man.

These two looked at each other for a while, the old Redman seeming sleepy enough to slide off and conk right there. After that short while was over though, the Indian spoke up.

"The small man is killed," he said in his rusty voice.

Lee Morgan sat looking at the old man, and said nothing. Bud Bent, watching, was amused, figuring that Lee was going to get the lesson in outwaiting that the old man had handed him—but not so. After a minute or two, the old Indian said, "Dowd."

Matthew Dowd. A little midget of a man. . . a great cattle-king and financier . . . husband to Catherine. A husband who had lost his wife to a legend, to Lee's father, Buckskin Frank Leslie.

And on her death, for whatever reason, the little man had befriended Lee, had helped him to a fortune, then sold Lee all the land of the Roughs in exchange for that fortune. Had helped him triple the size of Spade Bit.

Dead.

Killed.

A man too small to reach the floor with his feet while sitting in a chair.

Killed.

"Who killed Mister Dowd?" Lee said to the Indian.

"A white chief," the old Indian said, "and another man." He pronounced "another" the way a Frenchman might. *"Anozzer . . ."*

Lee had noted the old man's blanket.

"In Canada?"

"Canada . . . yes!" The Indian nodded vigorously. The old man had a powerful aroma to him; he smelled like a dog fox to the wranglers standing 'round.

Little Matthew Dowd had been a Canadian himself . . . had been up in the Canadian Rockies looking for pastureland on the grand scale. "Fourteen, fifteen thousand acres," he'd said to Lee six months before. "And that owned hard and fast. Ten times that land in leases and rights of way . . ."

A great deal of land for a small man to own, to control. Land all mountainous, all wild. Trappers' land, if anyone's at all.

"I feel," Dowd had said to Lee, both of them out at the yearling corral, looking at the young animals, considering a colt named Pompey as a possible stakes racer, "I feel that those wild lands in Saskatchewan hold much of the future for the cattle business . . . other businesses, as well."

"Furs?"

"No, son," Dowd had said, squinting behind his spectacles across the sun-struck corral (hazed now with kicked-up dust from the yearlings' play), "no, son—the fur trade is a tenth of the trade it was. Good enough for the odd trapper, not for great concerns. Beaver's done in big business.'' The little man had stood awkwardly, one small shoe-shod foot propped high on the fence's lowest rail (Lee had never seen Dowd at physical ease) stood stiffly propped thus, watching the horses. ''Brute land is the ticket,'' Dowd said. ''Great miles and miles of land—for cattle, for timber, for metals.''

''Fierce weather further up,'' Lee said. ''Even fiercer than Idaho's.''

''The colder the sea, the richer the fishery,'' the little man said, squinting, smiling up at Lee as if that tall, dangerous fellow, son of the killer who had taken Dowd's wife, were in some odd fashion a true son of Matthew Dowd as well.

''Well, it's your country, after all,'' Lee had said, as they turned away to walk back to the headquarters house and Sunday dinner.

''No,'' Dowd said to him, tripping along as well as he could to keep pace with Lee's shortened strides. ''No, my country was Victoria—warm and on the sea. Those mountains up there might as well be on the moon, for my familiarity. I have my reports, of course; I mean from my personal knowl-edge . . .''

They'd had a lamb stew for dinner, an oddity Lee had bought from a herder past the Old Man, butchered-out and cooked by McCorkle in a gentle style. It had tasted well enough, cooked with wild onions, mint and thyme. The lamb, roasted potatoes, and lima beans. Iced cream made with fine-ground vanilla for their dessert.

The little man had enjoyed it and had jokingly offered McCorkle a hundred dollars a week to come and cook for him.

"I hear you got a sissy Frenchman already, making you sauce messes, Mister Dowd," McCorkle said, spooning out the iced cream. "I'll not be taking another man's place, and him a poor foreigner without the gift."

That afternoon, little Dowd had buggied out and off of Spade Bit, sided by a Chicago gunman named Harrison, a pleasant, dangerous fat man, and a friend to Dowd, as well as a servant.

Lee had never seen the little man again— would never see him, now—and had had no word from him, either.

The loss he felt was surprising, Dowd having, after all, been not that much to him . . . had, it was true, done Lee favors, though never to his own loss. Had, it was also true, called Lee "son," and appeared in some sort to mean it. Had, most of all, been someone who had *known* . . . . had known Catherine as his wife, had known Lee's father, had hired that gentle man-killer on as some sort of regulator.

Had *known* them.

Had met S'ien too, once, up in Parker. Had seen Lee walking with her down Corduroy

Street, arm in arm, laughing, just as if she were white, paying no heed to the looks they were getting . . .

Dowd had seen them from his carriage—he was in Parker on railroad shipping business— had had his Jehu pull the horses up, had jumped down into the dust and come trotting over to the boardwalk and up the steps to say "good day" to them both, take the Chinese girl's hand, and bow his snappy little bow to her like a small boy's at a dancing class.

For that notice, that kindness, amid a street of stares—for that small, snappy bow to her, Lee felt some considerable loss.

Some . . . duty.

He sat on the pile of sawn timber, watching the old Indian as the old Indian was watching him.

"Are you a Cree? That your tribe?"

The old man nodded slowly as a turtle might have. Lee saw that the Redman was near done in for all his sturdy dignity, his silences, his scornful airs. It would have been a long, long ride down into this country. A dangerous ride for a Redman . . . And likely no great ease before, in whatever violence had finally come to little Matthew Dowd and killed him.

The old man stunk of campfire smoke, animal grease, and sweat. The pee-stink of an old man was in there, too. But most of all, he smelled of tired.

There'd be time enough to hear how Dowd

had died. To decide what to do about it—if anything there was to be done.

"What's your name? The one any man can say?"

The old man pursed his withered lips, deciding whether to answer this personal a question. It took him a while, deciding.

"I called by 'Stone-Made-Shining-by-Water.'"

Lee spoke to Bud Bent. "Take old Pebble here down to headquarters; let him wash in a horse trough if he's a mind, tell McCorkle to feed him, and bunk him down in the stable. Keep him put. I'll be down and talk with him tomorrow."

The hands listening grinned at the sight of Bud Bent in the role of nursemaid to a nasty old Red nigger, nudged each other, and waited to see what Bent would say to that order.

And he might have said plenty, have said that he killed Indians (when they crossed him), and didn't wipe their dirty butts for them no matter what, no matter who said "hop!" Might have said that and had more than enough sand to say it but, annoyed that the other wranglers expected some such noise, decided to disappoint them.

"Shit," he said. And to the Cree, "Come on along with me, you old shite-poke." Then reined his horse around and trotted off, not waiting to see if the old man followed. But Pebble, (known as that from then on) had caught the drift and kicked up his little nag and shambled after, a shriveled satellite to burly old Bent and his fine deep-chested bay.

With Bud and his Indian gone, the wranglers were eager to remark on the matter—on Dowd's death, particularly. Wasn't every day a cattle king worth millions of dollars got himself snuffed like some ragged-ass drover drunk and shot behind a whorehouse.

They would liked to have discussed it, just for a time, before getting back to sawing and stacking (poor work for a horse-man, in any case), but Lee turned a cold face and a colder eye on the first remark or two, and the hands sighed and ambled back to the saw-pit, plank piles, and lumber wagon, reflecting that the Bit was getting to be a fierce horse ranch to work.

The next day at midmorning, Lee rode into headquarters and found the old Indian sitting singing on the cook-shack steps. The song was a toneless Indian thing, but the old man quavered it with considerable feeling and didn't appear abashed at Lee's pulling up his big grey by the steps to listen.

The old Cree, McCorkle later informed Lee, had taken a scrub and wash in a corral horse trough (and had rolled and splashed and spouted with pleasure while doing it). He had also, both the evening before and this morning, eaten enough food for any two young men. "Swallowed like a snake," McCorkle said, "and kept every bit of it down."

Lee sat his grey listening to the old man for a while, then dug into his buckskin jacket pocket for a Grover House cheroot, broke it in half, tossed one half to the old Redskin, and scratched a lucifer on his boot sole to light up the other for himself. Old Pebble broke off his singing abruptly, on neatly catching the tossed butt, and stood up to stand at the grey's shoulder for a light. The old man then sucked on the cigar end like a child with candy drop. Smoke wreathed his head in a moment, appearing to come out of his ears.

Lee swung down off the grey, dropping the reins to ground-tie, and hunkered down beside the old man on the steps, to sit quiet and smoke.

They both had smoked their cigar halves down to stubs and no word spoken, when the old man turned to Lee and said, "You know this Lake Leboarde?" For a moment, Lee didn't understand him; (*'Lac Leboorduh'* it sounded like.) Then, he did.

"It's up in the 'Tooths?' Up in Saskatchewan?"

"Yes!" the old man said, pleased. "It is in *Les Dents,* the Tooth Mountains." He pinched out the last embers of his cigar stub, popped the wad of tabacco into his mouth, chewed and swallowed it. "There is big woods there, in the mountains. Son-of-bitch big woods. Son-of-bitch big mountains!" He burped, mouth wide and innocent. It was a long, satisfying burp, with nothing of civilization in it. Then the old man sat quiet.

Lee sat quiet as well. Bent to grind out his cigar butt, and sat still, content to let the old Indian's story come leaking out as it would.

It was some time before Pebble said anything more. Time enough for them to watch the stable hand, a boy named William Lerfer, drive the manure wagon past them, park it at the stables, get down, and commence shoveling out the dung heap beside the stable's west doorway.

They watched for a while, then the old Indian said, "I old. Old man. I have no strength not to be afraid to die." Lee said nothing, and the old man didn't either, for some time. Then he said, "White Chief Surrey come and argue with the Small Man at Lake Leboarde. Then he go away."

Lee was considerable surprised to see that the old Cree had begun to cry. Indians cried, of course, like any people, and had more reason than most. But it was unusual all the same.

"I no young man," the old Cree said. His cheeks were so deeply scored by weather-lines and wrinkles that the tears perforce ran down these channels. "Too old to fight." He shook his head, looking more shriveled than ever. "Too old to fight." Looked up at Lee.

"For to guide! Small Man pay me for to guide —not fight!"

Lee said nothing.

"At night, owl call three times. Chief Surrey come into camp with slave. Then, Jacques Forge come.

"Small Man come out, speak to them. Chief Surrey shoot in his heart . . ." Here, Pebble rubbed his stomach, where Indians believed the heart to lie, until the fear of death raised it higher. "Shoot him and say 'You be long time dying for that.' "

No more tears now; the old man had run out of them.

"I too old to fight," the Cree said. "I crawl away like old dog. Crawl on belly away like old dog . . ."

"Harrison," Lee said. "What of Harrison?"

The old man didn't appear to know the name.

"The fat man, with the round hat and the big revolver."

The old Cree wiped his nose on his right wrist, and nodded mournfully. "Mister Biscuit Man. He was good man—he would fight." The old man made a clicking sound with his tongue against his toothless gums. "That Forge went first into Biscuit Man's tent—" the Cree made a swift gesture across his throat. "Kill him. Then, when White Chief Surrey go—Forge, he put Biscuit Man into fire. Cook him. Eat him."

Lee took the last with more than a grain of

salt. Indians told the truth as children told it, sometimes. The truth as they wished it to be. He'd heard of cannibals right enough, trappers wintered in and starving . . . Liver-eatin' Johnson, a few others. Likely, though, the old man was making monsters out of murderers to excuse his crawling out of camp when the trouble came.

Surrey . . . and *Jacques Forge.* Seemed to him he'd heard something of a trapper up in Canada named Forge. Someone up in Spring Fork talking about the man . . .

In any case, Lee doubted Pebble was lying about those names. Names were important to Indians.

Surrey . . . and Jacques Forge. Must be some punkin's, to think they could kill Matthew Dowd and step out untouched. Millionaires didn't die quietly. Their funerals were followed by a parade of police and lawyers and politicians. Some punkin's, to murder Matthew Dowd . . . And to cut Harrison's throat for him, in the bargain. That fat Chicago hoodlum had been getting on, but he'd still been tough as a nail-keg and quick with a revolver, for all his fat.

"The Small Man breathed for a day and a night. I saw. I watch. He lie in the grass. Call for water to drink. White Chief is gone . . . and by next time night come, Small Man does not call for water to drink, but he still breathes. Forge stays; he cooks; he eats; then he take big piece of Biscuit Man—" the old

35

man patted his left leg; "—and he go away."

Lee thought that perhaps the old man hadn't lied about Jacques Forge after all.

"I come out from big woods. Get water. But Small Man cannot drink no more. He go 'psss-psss-psss.' " The old man made the sound of whispering.

"He tell me go get Morgan from Spade Bit, in States Idaho, and now I do it. Men do shit to me when I ride down! They throw rock— say *dirty nigger, go away!* But I am no son-of-bitch dog! I come here where Small Man say to come!" Darker color had flushed into the old man's face.

"You did well, Pebble," Lee said. "You are a good Indian."

"Yes, I am! I am a good Cree Indian. I am a Squirrel!"

Lee supposed that was his clan.

"Small Man was taking too long dying, and was unhappy. It was I hit him on his head with a stick so that he died."

"That . . . was well done," Lee said, after a moment.

"I am old but I am still a man," the Indian said.

Lee said nothing more for a while, but sat and thought, the Indian silent beside him. Lee thought about what was to be done on the ranch—the timbering, and building-work, the yearlings to be sold, the hoof-and-mouth theatening from the south.

His small place in Montana, the Rifle

River, could use a visit. A good little place . . . but could use a visit.

"I'll be riding north to Canada," he said to the old man. "You may stay here, if you wish, or come with me." A fool for sure, on a fool's errand . . .

"Not stay!" the Indian said. "Cree is Canada Indians! Not States' Indians! Our father is across the sea!"

"All right, then," Lee said, "we ride together—and likely to set both of our asses in a brace."

The old Cree appeared pleased at this, and smacked his lips to indicate agreement.

"An old fool and a young fool," Lee said. "That seems to suit."

CHAPTER TWO

They rode out the morning of the next day early, at still dark.

Ford, the wiry, pint-sized little tough who stood as Lee's foreman on the place, had not seemed surprised when Lee'd told him he was traveling north. "Want company?" he'd said. "Sefton?" Sid Sefton—black-haired, sleek and handsome, fast with his revolver. Good with the horses, too. Gentle.

"No, I'll take no man. Just go back up with the Cree."

"That old nigger'll be no more use than a fart in a high wind."

"I don't figure on much trouble."

Ford had stood straight in his fancy high-top Texan boots, full five-and-a-half feet in them if he was an inch. He had a face like a fighting rooster's, brown and beaked. Lee had always felt the wrangler had owl-hooted something considerable in his time. "You're a damn liar," Ford said, "but it's your look-out."

"That's right," Lee said. "My look-out. You just take care of the place for me. And for Christ's sake, watch for that hoof-and-mouth!"

In the cool darkness of morning, Lee rose in the headquarters house, empty but for him, dressed, packed his war-bag, buckled on the Bisley Colt's, and slid his broad-bladed dagger down into its sheath in his right boot. "You're a damn liar . . ." Ford had said.

True enough. True enough . . .

Making little Dowd's death his excuse to go killing?

Lee hoped to God that that was not so. He was surely not so much a beast as that . . .

He shouldered his war-bag and walked out onto the back porch to the ice-box, raised the thick oak lid, and fished down into the cold water, the drifting chunks of ice, for the corked stone jug of buttermilk. Opened it, took a long drink of the frigid sour sweetness. Plugged the jug and put it back. And remembered, for an instant, S'ien dead in her glittering shroud of ice.

Never had thought for a moment that she would die . . . it had never occurred to him. Never occurred to him . . .

He walked back through the house, took the big Sharps down from above the fireplace, and went on out the front door. The moon was down . . . no stars at all. Wouldn't be long now, maybe an hour before the sun came up. A chill on the morning, too. Winter on its way . . . would be winter pretty soon up in those Canadian mountains.

That cold, that deep snow, might have kept her looking alive.

Forever . . . ?

The old Cree was sitting his horse just past the porch, waiting.

No rackety little pinto, now; Lee had traded him even for a big-barrelled paint named Patches. A stayer, if not much of a goer. Patches was twice the horse the other had been, but old Pebble had muttered darkly about the trade, and made half-hearted gestures of refusal. Not trusting bargains with whites, apparently. Not even very good bargains.

Lee had intended tacking out his big grey, but the old Indian was already working guide, it seemed. The grey shifted restless at the rail, Lee's Brazos double-rig already cinched on, tacked from noise to tail with Lee's leather. The old man had kept his eyes open, his two days at Spade Bit.

A big brown named Butch was lead-roped behind the Cree's paint, packed up in neat diamond-hitches. The old man appeared to know his business.

Lee went down the steps to his horse, checked the girth—the grey would wind, if he got the chance—then slid the Sharps into the rifle-boot, tied his war-bag on behind the cantle, slipped the reins from the rail, and swung up into the saddle.

Lamps were lit in the bunk-house out past the yearling corral. Hands would be up and doing, heading to the cook-shack for fried steak and eggs, biscuits and molasses. Spade Bit breakfasted big and suppered small.

No need for fare-thee-wells.

"Pebble," Lee said, "you lead the packy," and turned the grey's head north.

Some fare-thee-well, after all. As they jog-trotted out past the tool shed, McCorkle came hot-footing it through the fading dark with a tied up bundle—burlap over oiled paper it felt like, as he handed it up to Lee—and said, "Some chow-chow an' shit for the trail," turned at that, and went hot-footing back up to the path to his cooking. There, at the lamplit door of the cook-shack, Lee saw Charlie Potts and Sid Sefton standing, tin coffee cups in their hands. They raised the cups to him, and Lee saw Sefton grin.

Some fare-thee-well, after all.

Lee lifted his hand to them, and spurred the grey out.

They passed the wire store, with its stink of spoiled grease and rust, then jogged on into the north field, pasture for the brood mares and colts in season. Fallow now, the last of the moonlight frosting the dew-wet grass. The morning smelled clean as new paper—if that paper had been cold pressed out of green pine, green willow, the yellow-brown grass of autumn. Cold pressed and riffled out still cold in the moonlight.

Lee felt a little better than he had felt in some time. Felt as if the weight that had borne down upon him, that had lain across his shoulders like a ox yoke since the girl had died, was easing, was easing just the least little bit.

"I pray to God," Lee said to himself, "that it might be so." He moved his shoulders as a man might under the lessening of a true weight of stone or timber or metal. "I have been sick in grief," he thought, "but I will be getting better." And thought that he would have been better already if he had been man enough to have told her what she meant to him . . . to have married her in church like a Christian person, instead of visiting her like a whore . . . fucking her like a whore. He could have married her, brought her to Spade Bit, and God help the man who had a word to say about it but "congratulations."

Then, she would have been down here, not in Parker, when the diptheria came.

Down here. Back at the house still asleep, likely, curled naked . . . soft ivory. Warm as toast. Would have wished him a quiet farewell last night, hugged him hard enough to break a rib.

Loved him. Quimmed all the lonely out of him, then slept in the circle of his arms. He would be riding out now, thinking only of riding back.

That was the way it would have been.

Oh, yes . . . that was the way it would have been.

The grey was showing his fault—shying at dawn breezes come rustling from the dark. He was a tall, knacky creature, late cut, powerful and fast. But the possession of his balls quite late had left him discontented somewhat, nervous, ill-at-ease at sudden motions, sounds.

Lee let him sidle here and there for a few moments, then slid his crop out of his left boot-top and batted the grey smartly between the ears. The horse crow-hopped, farted, and settled down to its swinging, reaching stride. Lee heard the old Cree's paint break into a fast trot behind him, the pack-horse trotting as well to keep up.

Past the pine grove . . . a good-bye of pine scent, of wind whispers. Then up beyond the north meadow, the horses' withers heaving at the climb. Steep country, every which way a man traveled. Could be steep country for a man sometimes even on the flats.

They nooned in the Roughs. Spade Bit land now, damn few squatters left, and those only shadows of men drifting across the country to hole up in a brake, to slaughter a beef or colt for feasting before starvation swung in again. Drifters who drifted mighty light, who flitted like fair-tale creatures, ducking the weight of Spade Bit's strong arm. The rope ends, the boots—and the whip.

Only a man already more than half mad could dream through a beating at the hands of the wranglers—or worse, a beating at Lee Morgan's hands—and men that mad, that dreamy with drifting, were usually left alone, only shoved on their way.

The Roughs were tamed.

Old Pebble cooked up coffee about as quick as Lee had ever seen it done, and though it wasn't any equal of McCorkle's brew, still a man could drink it and find some satisfaction.

The Cree had cooked it to almost a boil in a cracked tin pot on a handful of busted twigs, caught the loose grounds with the heel of his hand as he poured the hot stuff out into cups as poorly founded as the pot, then had hunkered back with a grunt to drink his portion, toothless jaws champing, wrinkled lips sputtering as he sipped.

The morning had wakened bright as a penny, and now noon was as hot and full of light as autumn permitted, always allowing for the steady, slow, cool flood of air that rolled forever down the granite slopes of the Old Man to flow as steadily as a river might down the mountain pastures, the steep meadows stitched now with every dark yellow, every light brown that dying grass could show.

Lee hunkered as the old Indian did, drank his coffee, and looked out over the country. Nothing to be seen but mountains and mountain country, steeps and slides, the rich borders of willow and dwarf oak. The air and its light were clear as clear water, dotted in one place only by the distant hanging of a hawk. No sounds but the slow wind through the grass . . . the distant whistle of a marmot, doubtless warning any marmot fool of the shadow of that hawk.

Lee found he felt better than he had for some time.

"Say, you Pebble—this is prime coffee."

The old Indian glanced at him, surprised. Such praise of a man (for doing well what he ought to do well) was so white-skinned a thing that he never knew how to reply to it. It occurred to him, by no means for the first time, that a people who could so waste words must be very rich in them and need telegraph wires and heliographs to bear their burden.

Lee finished his coffee, waited impatiently for the old man to finish his, then stood, caught up the grey, mounted and rode, riding as a man does from unpleasantness to pleasure, however odd that seemed in the circumstances. An observer sitting his horse higher on the mountain slope would, even at some distance, have seen that horseman eager to travel, light in the saddle and leaning forward as he rode. That same observer could then have seen how quickly an old

Indian could break a noon-day camp, toss out grounds, tap out the cups, thrust pot and cups under a canvas flap in the pack-horse's diamond hitch, stride bow-legged to a barrel-chested paint, scramble aboard, and kick on out after the white man's lead—the pack horse, shaking it heavy head to shift a late season fly, trailing along at the end of its painter.

As they threaded the brakes through the afternoon stopping once for pissing, Lee and the old Cree passed two small horse-herds, Spade Bit range stock, hard and wiry as any Texas mustangs but showing their breeding, the Morgan blood, the strains of Barb and Thoroughbred, in deep, broad chests, short backs, haunches bunched with muscle. Their legs were fine as foxes.

Two hands, Shoenfeldt and Hardy, were duty wranglers in this section, and Lee would have been happier to have seen hide or hair of them as he and Pebble rode through. Still, they might well be off about their duties—heading strays, shooting wolves . . . doctoring. They might be, and they had better be. The Bit didn't pay top wages to loafers. Time enough when he got back to check the style of Shoenfeldt and Hardy. If these high herds were short-count in the tally, then those two would pay the difference one way or another.

Lee would certainly have liked to have seen at least one of those boys working. Hated to think he'd fallen so in despondency

47

that he'd hire or let Ford hire two lame ducks instead of prime hands.

Still . . . might not be so. Might be away chousing or hunting for the pot. Doctoring.

Be fair . . . that might be so.

The riding now was as rough as maybe—no sooner lunging up a steep, than a break-away would present itself fit to snap a horse's fores. Tangles were dense enough up here to claw a rider half off his mount, then strike him across the face as he straightened. It was harsh, tiring work for men and horses, and, mindful of the Cree's age, Lee would from time to time look behind him to see how old Pebble was faring. Each such look was returned by the old man directly—the pitch-black eyes, sunk deep in wrinkled sockets, as alert, untiring, incurious as ever. So far, the old man was well. How well he would remain after another day's riding, and then a week's riding and then *another* week's riding (and all these retracing the long journey he had already accomplished) was yet to be seen.

Up into the mountains of Canada. A fair piece of fine weather . . . something less than fair in foul. They were riding into winter, and winter coming down to meet them.

That night, at dusk, when the light had become leg-break, Lee pulled the weary grey up beside a stand of fir midway down a long, long ridge of such pines that flanked a mountain called The Grand, standing seventeen miles west of Parker, and looming over the horse-shoe loop of track the Northern Pacific had laid through Pashoka Pass.

Lee could see far below the glimmer of steel where the twin threads went snaking through the gorge. Supposed to have lost a number of dancers and layers to slides and faults, putting the line through. Hard to see how that was much of a shame . . .

Railroads were good for shipping stock. Good for business in general. Difficult to like that machinery, though. Unpleasant (except for the fine Harvey dinners) to ride those close and sweat-smelling cars, all coal smoke, and grease-spotted velvet . . . stranger's voices . . . opinions . . . their farts.

Bad memories for railroading. Perhaps those memories had spoiled these wonders for him. That mad Indian sometimes still loomed in dreams, his eyes bitten out by the whip. A merry little man in a banker's suit stood by smiling, killing Lee's father.

Dreams with the sound of locomotives in them. Gunshots . . .

It seemed to Lee, beside all that, that the railroads, like cavalry sabers, were slicing the country apart, wounding it.

He and the old Cree had ridden near a passenger train late that afternoon, one of those Northern Pacific trains, heading into Parker. They'd met it on wide flat, riding through deep, dry, and dying grass. The first breath of winter's cold seemed to flow across that flat, drifting down from the north.

They hadn't seen the tracks, the grass had been too deep, but the line of telegraph poles and wire marked where the tracks must run. Blackbirds had been perched on the wires in long rows, their feathers ruffling slightly in the wind gusts—the yellow-brown grass bending to those same gusts as if they, too, were feathers, the feathers of the round earth itself.

Lee had dug into his war-bag, pulled the coils of the blacksnake whip free, shook them out, and practiced swinging the long, slim, braided lash, sending the whip loops out to snap off withered blossoms among the sedge with reports as sharp as pistol fire. This whipwork had impressed the Cree as nothing else had, and he watched from the saddle as his paint trotted along, and now and then, at some particularly acute stroke, had stretched his mouth wide open in astonishment, like a child, and covered it with a dark brown, veiny, and wire-muscled hand.

They had seen the train's smoke before they heard its engine, the rumble of its wheels on steel; the wind had carried the sounds away from them as it stretched the stack smoke out to the south, blowing it down almost to the level of the grass.

Lee and the Cree had pulled up, eased their reins for their horses' gazing, and waited to see the monster pass.

It rolled by close enough to smell. Hot steel, coal smoke, dark, friction-heated oil. As the small square windows shuttled past, Lee saw the passengers—the men in small round-brimmed hats, suit coats or shirt sleeves, the women in picture hats, white shirtwaists grey with soot. These people looked at him, and especially at old Pebble, in his dirty Canada blanket, his bent-brimmed deerhide hat, the two red feathers he had stuck in the hatband.

They looked at Lee and the old Indian as if they were something to notice in a raree show. Objects of interest . . . but not much.

It occurred to Lee that the old Rocky Mountain beaver trappers must have been looked at much that same way, sixty, seventy years before, when the toughs from Texas and Kansas—young, cruel, full of piss and vinegar—came driving their cattle through all the wild country, talking of tallies and cash.

And likely, the Blackfeet and Crow had felt the impact of that mildly interested gaze when they, years earlier, had received it from those same mountain men, come singing through the passes with their pack trains, steel traps, and iron barreled Hawkin rifles.

"I am going out," he thought, *and these people are coming in.* His father had had the best of it . . . the best of times in this country. Had died as the old wild ways were dying. What would there have been for Buckskin Frank Leslie, had he lived? Life as an aging

rancher—loved, to be sure—but the prey of every newspaper man, every curiosity seeker, every stupid bully-boy come seeking something from him.

Lee wondered, as he had wondered before, if his father had tried his fastest, that day in the Spade Bit cook-shack. If he had tried his fastest, or had not. Seeing that small madman, perhaps, as a sort of manner of bowing out, a kind of curtain call, as people in theatricals said it.

Of course, he was not the man he had been —must have been slower. Perhaps he had drawn his fastest, perhaps had held his second shot (that used, Lee had heard, to follow the first so fast no listener could tell a space between) through some miscalculation. Perhaps had done his best after all, and had not longed for death . . .

Lee and old Pebble sat their horses, watching the railroad train go by. Three men had been sitting out on the small observation deck behind the caboose, smoking their pipes; they regarded Lee and the Indian gravely as the car drew past but made no motion of greeting. It was as if, Lee thought, he and the Cree were illustrations in *Harper's Weekly*, and not living men riding living animals. The men looked at them, puffed on their pipes, and were carried steadily past and away—seeming, so deep was the grass, to be carried magically through the prairie, the gleaming tracks lying buried under myriad wind-burned stalks.

A good reason, it seemed to Lee, for those Missouri men to have gone to robbing railroad trains. Difficult to consider a man as only landscape when he was aboard and had a long-barrel .44 presented to your head.

But rob them . . . blow the damn tracks up . . . heat the rails and twist them. All too late. Dancing of cannibal kings to conquer the rifles of the whites. Ghost dancing, and of as little use.

He swung down from the grey, loosed the cinch, heaved the saddle and his war-bag, caught the hobbles the old Indian tossed to him, and knelt to buckle them on. So fine legs this animal had—fair and fine cut. Reaching legs, for a run. Perhaps just a shade too fine for rough steep-country work.

Lee slipped the grey's bridle and slapped the horse's rump as it pranced by. Still some gumption . . .

The deep shade of the firs shadowed off into evening darkness. Far to the west, past Parker, Lee could see the last of sunlight rest red-gold along the peaks of the Rockies. The scent of the firs was rich upon the evening winds that cooled him, stirred the buckskin fringe along his jacket. Lee felt the riding sweat at the seat of his wool trousers grow cool against his butt, the heat of the day below drift away and beyond him into a chilling night.

The old Cree had already started his cook-fire—quick at trail-camp, for all his age. Appeared to be a fine hand at this sort of thing. Too bad little Dowd hadn't taken some young roughs along when he went north. The fat Chicago gunman hadn't been quick enough. This old man, nothing now but a good fire-maker, a packer, a camp cook . . .

Foolish Dowd—to go into enemy country so undefended.

Too many years spent rich, above all danger, all threat. Should have recalled that there was no perfect safety. Might not have cared, though, after Catherine died. Might not have cared enough to have regulators with him up in the north woods, when the killers came down with autumn.

Lee, feeling the riding stiffness now that he was cool (looking to see the ghost outline of the grey, the brighter-hided paint beside him gazing upslope of the firs) walked straight-legged, butt-sprung, to the Cree's fire. The old man was patting cornmeal cakes, forming them in his dirty, thin old hands and pausing now and then to add some canteen water gurgling to the mix. He'd propped a flitch of bacon on a sharp stick beside him and the tin pot was already cooking coffee in the coals.

A handy old Redskin at a campfire, no doubt about that.

Lee'd known worse traveling company. Much worse.

He hunkered across the fire feeling that bent-knee crouch pull the saddle-ache out of the long muscles of his thighs and watched across the fire as the old man worked. Pebble had made an Indian fire, small and pyramidal. Association with whites hadn't spoiled his fire-making, then.

The sparks from some damp twig went sputtering, snapping, popping up into the blackening air between them. Fountaining up, pouring up into the dark in a bright little sudden stream, as if they had a where to go.

The firs were talking where the wind came through. A cool wind, getting colder.

A pine grove, Lee thought, was no bad place to lie, asleep or dead. *Sleep well . . .* he said silently to his dead girl. *Won't be too long, surely. Not too many long years . . . and I'll be with you.*

Nine days later they crossed the line. Lee would never have known it (they were leading the horses across a confounded slope of scrub pine and shale scree) except that old Pebble, puffing and scrambling behind, suddenly called out *"En Canada!"* This was not, at the moment, great news, Lee believing that Canada scree was as likely to crack a horse's cannon as any other uncertain stone.

It had grown colder in the week and more of riding, colder and higher and thicker with trees.

In that week, Lee had seen confirmed his

good opinion of the old Cree as camper. Pebble had shot prairie hen and grouse for the pot with his crack-stocked shotgun and then cooked them near as well as McCorkle might have. He had been infallible at camp sets and horse care. He had kept still and his mouth shut, except for a few odd songs.

And he had kept up despite his age.

It was on one of the grouse shooting occasions that the old Indian had seen Lee fire the Bisley Colt's.

Pebble had sudddenly whipped his paint forward, yipping more like a Comanche than a northern forest Indian, and had stirred and started a covey of grouse up out of the autumn-bitten brush. The birds had exploded left and right, up and sideways as was their style. And rattled as they flew.

The old man had taken a going-away bird with his right barrel, missed with his left.

Lee had drawn and shot that grouse as it rose thirty feet above him and turning. The bird fell like a stone, its feathers shredding into deep brown grass. This sudden shot—most remarkable, even for the lucky shot that it surely was—did not startle the old man as Lee's whip practice had. That doing with the whip, the Cree had regarded as extraordinary. This stunning revolver draw-and-shoot, the accuracy of which surprised Lee himself —it was the odd, unlikely end result of dour months in the hills after S'ien's death . . . endless practice at pine-stobs, cones, twigs—

this the old man considered merely magic. He had seen Lee draw the pistol once before, at a sudden breaking of a high willow branch when they camped above a river whose name the Cree didn't know. It had been dark then, but Lee had turned and drawn the revolver in firelight, and Pebble had seen that action clearly. He saw it, and it was apparent to him that Lee had paid a shaman very well indeed for such a magical and enchanted weapon which leaped at his slightest motion from his holster to his hand.

At that time, of course, the old Cree believed that only the weapon was enchanted—he had, to be sure, seen many superb riflemen, had been more than a fair handler of weapons himself, and had known men very handy with revolvers. But this was in a different category. And now, after this shot that had struck the spinning grouse in midair, Pebble knew that Lee must have spent many many horses for magic bullets as well.

He was impressed by such great wealth and impressed even more that Lee should have used it only to purchase this magical weapon and its bullets and not for more serious gifts, such as the ability to turn into a crow and fly straight to heaven to roost on the arm of God.

Lee dismissed that shot for what it was—a fluke—put the Bisley away (it was a fairly new weapon, shipped from Connecticut in the spring; he had shot the screws out of the previous piece with all his practicing) and thought no more about it.

Thought no more about being in Canada, either.

Time enough for that when they got near *Eustache*, a settlement of trappers and merchants. Woods-runners. Back of beyond, from what little sense he could make out of old Pebble. Dowd had gone out from there to the mountains just west of Banf, a hopeful railroad town, apparently, and to his death.

Time enough, then, to think about being in Canada. Looking ahead, across the scree slope, the scrub pines, seemed to him that Canada looked just as rough and west and high as Idaho did and the slab of Montana they'd had to cross. Never seemed to him there was much to Canada. Furs . . . those Louis Riel people. Damned if he knew why those people were content to keep kissing England's ass—though maybe they'd gotten tired of that by now, had their own parliament or whatever.

The grey was weary of the broken shale; it danced sideways, skittering on the fractured rock. Lee kept a good hold on the reins, hauling the horse half up once when it slipped.

Heavy damned horse.

The announcement of Canada appeared to have inspired the Cree, who now commenced to sing one of his unwieldy songs, all Redskin groans and grunts.

The grey didn't like the noise, either.

"Shut up," Lee said, and Pebble shut.

Past the slope, the country fell away into a creek valley as sudden and deep as any Lee had seen. This narrow gulch was thick with trees as a wolf with fur—thick enough, it looked, to ride across the canyon on, as if it had been a plank floor—but green and fronded. It looked no more a pleasure to travel in truth than the scree slope had been. Busted knees for a rider, it looked like, if those trees grew as close as they looked.

Lee led the grey out to the level shelf, a stretch of rough gravel left by some avalanche, and swung up into the saddle. He waited until Pebble came jobbing up on his paint—the pack-horse, looking worn, head hanging, trotting heavily behind.

Lee pointed out over the creek valley. "We go through that?"

The old Cree, nodding a "no," (nodding was "no," head-wagging was "yes" among the northern tribes) said, "We go all around down there. No through."

Around was damn sure better than through, and Lee waved the old man and his led pack horse into the lead, touched the grey with his spurs to follow.

The trail down—a long, steep, notched cut was more what it was—did indeed wind "all around" as it pitched down alongside the gulch. The day's weather was chill, cloud-mottled; the sun, pale as the moon and hiding. No wind, though. The air, full of the smell of cold stone and pine, was still, heavy, cold as cold water. The sounds of their horses' hooves rang and clattered off the fractured granite that sided them closely as they rode down the side of the mountain. No-Name Mountain, apparently; at least Pebble had no name for it. A measure, Lee supposed, of the wildness, the loneliness of this north country, that great mountains and considerable rivers as well went unnamed, existed only as gigantic accidents, features of a greater wilderness.

Lee heard some small animals chattering, moving through the tangled growth to their right. They had descended below the tops of the trees and staring deep into the growth, Lee saw that the stand of trees was thick enough to crowd out daylight, to drown the light in dense row on row of tight packed trunks and tangled foliage. And these were big trees, not bare-bone lodgepole. Hundreds of them—maybe thousands—all crowded into this narrow, deep cut, not more than three-quarters of a mile long.

Lee reined the grey left, closer to the rock face. Still a good hundred-foot drop to the right, the army of tall pines marching down the mountain beside them. It was possible that Dowd had been chasing the wrong rainbow up here, going for ranch land and mine-metals. Seemed to Lee that timber might have been a better bet. Need to have your stands near good running water, of course, to raft your cut logs out . . .

Certain sure he wouldn't have been the first man to have thought of that, despite all the unnamed mountains, the unnamed rivers. These might not be named, but what was of value was surely marked down on maps in Toronto or wherever. Marked down in New York City, too, and Boston. Money people in fine business offices ordering their sissy secretaries to bring them this paper or that. Odd people . . . but tougher, crueler and harder men in their way than any horn-handed wrangler could ever be.

Lee saw Pebble pull his paint up ahead and climb slowly down from the saddle. Looked to be a sudden dip there—and was; Lee saw the old Indian climb down out of sight, rein-tugging the paint and pack-horse down after him. Lee stepped down and led the grey to follow. The pack horse wasn't going well— stepping as heavy as Barnum's elephant. Hard to understand that. Most packies picked up as a trailing went along and their loads lightened. Hate to think the damn animal was wind-broken. Some humiliating, to raise fine horses and choose out a lunger to travel.

The dip was a sudden drop and slide—at least fifteen feet, and so steep a man could barely keep his footing. Littered with stones the size of steers' heads, among a few dozen more as big as baseballs. The grey came down almost sitting on his rump, eyes walled, in a tattoo of nervous farts. Lee had to skip pretty light to stay clear of the animal's fore-hooves. As he got the grey down to damn-near-level, Lee glanced up to see old Pebble, already a good way down the track, mounted, easy in his saddle, the paint and packy well in hand, gazing back at him with the satisfied expression of a man well finished with a sticky, watching a companion not quite out of it.

Lee tried to mount the grey, but the animal shied away from him and came within a step of the trail-edge, so Lee stepped back and hauled hard on the reins. This god-damned hammer-head was going to kill himself—kill both of them, if he didn't look out!

"Now, hold hard, you son-of-a-bitch!" Lee held the reins with his right hand and hit the grey between the eyes with his left fist. He hit him as hard as he could, and the grey grunted, gave slightly at the knees, and was afterward calmer.

This seen, and the hauling and scrambling that followed, (the level sank at once to another steep dip) appeared to give some satisfaction and amusement to the old Cree, who as a guide had no doubt seen many mossy-horns make fools of themselves in strange country. For one mountain was not at all like another, and a strange country was more different than that, even to the lie of its stones.

Lee persevered, dragged the reluctant grey out of the second pit, and found the true level beside the still-faced Indian. He mounted, blew out a windy breath of relief—nothing but a lightly sprained ankle, a lightly kicked leg to show for it. Damndest little slides he'd seen. Leg-break country, for sure.

"If I find," he said to the old man, "—if I find you took this track for funning, I will peel a strip of that red hide right off you."

Pebble nodded, and smiled a little smile.

Two days later, they saw a man riding.

Lee was leading up the center of a wide valley—an old river valley, it seemed—cut down its center by the stony living grass here, protected from the hard, cold north winds by mountains running north by east along the valley's side. The grass was alive, but not by much. It had the matted, burned look the plains grasses got as winter came down on them. Live enough for the horses' graze, in any case; still light green at the roots.

There were no trees in the mile-wide stretch of the valley, no thicket, no scrub. Only the cold-flattened grass, like an endless muddy carpet, lying creased, humped, folded shallowly here and there in its reach to the rising foothills, the mountains beyond.

Lee had been sewing on a shirt as he rode along—the flannel torn where the sleeve met the shoulder. He was looking to set his last few stitches, doubled at the place the sleeve had torn away, when he noticed the grey carrying his head a little high, and looked up to find the cause.

A speck on the near horizon just to the left of the line of the old river's bed. Moving speck. Moving.

Lee pulled the grey up, jammed shirt, needle, and thread into a saddle bag, and slid off, pulling the big Sharps up and out of its bucket as he went. The grass was deeper than it looked from horseback, came up to his thighs as he stood.

A rider out there. One.

Lee heard the old Cree grunt, climbing down from the paint. It might be a notion to lay the horses down; be a sight harder to spot in this grass.

"Can you see what that fellow is?"

Pebble said nothing for a moment, just making that clicking noise with his tongue. Lee looked back and saw the old man standing on one leg, the other bent-kneed as he scratched an ankle, and squinting hard at the distant rider. He stared for awhile, then curled up a hand as if it were a telescope, and peered through it.

"Metis."

"What?"

"Breed!" Pebble put his fresh-scratched leg

down into the grass, then hunched over, like an Indian riding, and gestured toward the horseman.

Lee supposed the Indian knew what the was talking about—this was his country—but damned if *he* could make out how the man over there was riding, and he a third the old man's age. *"Metis . . ."* Those would be the breed trappers who had followed old Riel—to the gallows, some of them.

No reason this man would cause them trouble. No reason—but still a maybe. Traveling, it was best to avoid strangers; might do you good to meet—more likely do you harm. Only one rider, though. Let him do the running.

"Let's ride." He reached up to slide the Sharps back into its bucket, then climbed onto the grey. Heard Pebble grunt his way aboard the paint. Old man must agree with his conclusion. The grey snorted, tossing his head, still getting the scent of a strange horse on the wind as Lee spurred him out to a canter.

Fellow wouldn't miss such doings, and would most likely haul his freight thereafter.

Lee heard another somewhere as he rode, thunder off to the north, the deep sound rolling and echoing off the mountain slopes at either side of the valley. No black cloud in the sky that he could see, just long silver fish-scales marching over them, moving slowly on a high wind. Must be storming miles and miles away, the sounds of it rolling down the range.

Lee saw the distant horseman more clearly now. He wore a cap instead of a hat, it seemed. Some sort of light-colored duster. Fellow rode a black horse.

He turned that horse's head as Lee watched. Decided to run then instead of coming on to try Lee and the old man out. Might think them road-agents or simply a pair of those wandering creatures that roamed here and there, seeking any sort of trouble or profit, however small.

Turning away. Riding toward the mountains to the south.

Lee didn't fault him for it, either—would, in fact, have skedaddled himself (old Cree, pack-horse, and all) if the rider had had companions.

Behind him, Lee heard the Cree began another of his songs, this one more tuneful than most. Lee assumed the old man was singing about this encounter, likely with considerable embroidery. Give the old man credit, he'd ridden even with Lee right along —better than even, sometimes. And this, doubling back on a long, hard ride he'd already made. A more than tough old man, and a true one, to come so far with Dowd's last words. Reason enough to respect an old man . . . to let him sing. Lee thought he had been wrong to tell the old man to shut up when he sang sometimes.

Let the old man sing. He was earning it. Didn't sound as bad as it had, anyway. Lee supposed he was getting used to it.

That night, they camped by a fast fall a few miles north of the dry-grass valley. They camped high, and went to some trouble getting up to the place; it seemed to Lee to be worth it, to get a down-hill stretch fc. the morning. And there was running water—a good deal better than the drain-hole stuff they'd been drinking and watering the horses with.

The stream (no name to it, as far as Pebble knew) broke down a mountainside through a granite trench nearly blocked at a number of places by fallen slabs of stone as big as houses. These foaming steps of falls and rapids sprayed fountains of icy water where they struck those blocking boulders in a sounding, ringing roar of noise as if to answer the distant thunder that still, at night-fall, echoed through the dark mountains from some far-away storm.

Lee and the Indian made their camp, and the Cree cooked a slumgullion stew rich and hot enough to stoke them against the wind that came whistling down with the falling river.

The stew, and coffee boiled over a heap of sticks Pebble had hoarded and bundled on the packy was followed by a smoke (Lee's last cheroot) sliced in half and shared, as they hunkered. Then, a while later, smoked out and weary, they rolled into buffalo robes, tucking well down out of the wind.

One of the great pleasures of trailing—being fed in empty wilderness, keeping warm in cold winds, lying safe in dangerous country . . .

As fat, tough Harrison had lain in Dowd's lonely camp. Fed . . . warm . . . thinking himself safe. Until the edge of the knife drew smoothly through his throat.

Lee lay beneath the weight of the robe, the dusty, raw-leather stink of buffalo, and thought about seeming safety for a while—then said *"Shit,"* shoved the warm folds of fur aside, sat up to jam on his boots, reached back into the robe for the Bisley Colt's, and stood up.

The cold soaked him like a thrown bucket of water.

It took quite a while to circuit the camp, the lay of the land was so rough, so up and down. It took more time also because Lee moved as quietly as he could over ancient heaps of water-dropped gravel, beds of pounded stone. He used his eyes in the shifting dark—the moon was still hidden behind peaks—used his ears, and his nose as well. It would be an odd man or group of men who didn't have some smelly to them after a long ride.

It took Lee a while to do this, to make his circuit slowly and thoroughly in the dark, the

Colt's ready, the double-edge dagger in his other hand.

Then he checked the horses. Unhappy and hobbled close, butts turned to the ceaseless wind. No sign from them that strangers were about—man or beast.

When satisfied, Lee sat tugging his boots off, looking out absently across the small river struggling in its trough, black as pitch except for those splashing spots where the coming moonlight barely touched it, he heard the old man cough, mutter, and then subside.

Hoped to god the Cree was not going sick on him. It was nothing to contemplate with pleasure, the notion of dragging a sick old man through this country. Likely was nothing but a Cree's comment on the noisiness of white man's quiet scout 'round the camp. Lee got his left boot off (always something of a struggle; a boot clerk in Butte had once told him all men had different-sized feet, right to left) then slid into the buffalo robe with a grunt of contentment. Any bad boys who hadn't found the camp while the fire was up and the stew cooking would be unlikely to find it now, deep full dark.

Buffalo. Had some up here, was told. Woods buffalo, something of that sort. Perhaps a chance for fresh hump . . . sight a fat cow and knock her down. Try that with wild onions . . . a can of tomatoes on the side.

A can of peaches to follow that. Be better than well-enough, that would.

Never a buffalo robe yet didn't stink to high heaven.

Warm, though—no man could say they weren't . . . .

Wolves woke Lee once, just before dawn. He lay listening to that chorus. What was it that vampire Count said in Mister Stoker's book? . . . *"Listen to them—the children of the night."* That was a book-and-a-half, that one was! 'Trash and manure,' Professor Riles would have called it. Poor Riles. Coughed his lungs up . . . that decent, wise man.

There were three wolves singing . . . maybe four, the real hundred-pound, throat-ruff, silver-tip timbers from the sound of them. A clever man could imitate a coyote's call pretty well, put lots of yapping into it; but not the sounds these articles made.

Lee turned deeper into the buffalo robe and seemed to slowly turn deeper still, into sleep. He didn't dream of S'ien.

CHAPTER THREE

Seven days later, in a fine, small fall of snow, they rode into *Eustache*. It had been a hard week's ride.

Pebble was sick, swaying in his saddle like a tired old toper. Had been sick and coughing since the night of the high camp, and had gotten sicker through the mountains. The third day from the damn camp, the old man had fallen off his paint and fainted when he tried to remount. Lee had nursed him through that night, cosying him in the robes, feeding him bits of rabbit and marmot with his fingers (the old man's toothless gums nibbling and sucking much, Lee thought, as a baby's must) and cleaning the old man's manure off his scrawny buttocks, much again, he thought, as he would have done with a little child.

Then—fed, cleaned, swaddled afresh in Lee's only clean shirt, Pebble had seemed to rest easier, to be cooler to the touch. Slept and snored a bit. Muttered, and crapped in Lee's shirt.

Then Lee regretted a dry camp, and wished mightily for that icy, thundering river with its spray-dashed stones. He also began to appreciate a portion of women's labors that had not previously occurred to him. Might be the poor souls spent much of their lives in that sort of cleansing. For himself, he was tempted to shoot the old native through the head and bury him briskly.

That night was the worst night for Lee, though the old man suffered from then on, weak, coughing, querulous. But he guided, and even, in tricky places, attempted to ride first, 'till Lee set him firmly back.

So they rode their seven days—Lee made slowly stronger and stronger by the weather and riding, the vigilance and meager food (shot conies and rabbits, mostly, but a few noosed), and Pebble, baking in fever, withering as he rode, shrinking, collapsing. The long ride down into Idaho had been, it seemed, the old Cree's last great effort. This ride—the long ride back into winter—was, after the misleading vigor of the start, killing him as surely as a Chippeway lance might have in bygone days.

Lee supposed he might have given the old man more rest before the start, perhaps have left him behind altogether. Might have done that, but hadn't. Too full of himself . . . of S'ien. Too busy with thoughts of what vengeance he would (like one of Riles's hero Greeks) wreak upon Dowd's killers.

Well, he was wreaking, all right. He was handing out death, for a start, to this old man. By carelessness. Yet, once on the trail, it was hard to see how it might have been better to hole up hungry in winter mountains. As it was, they rode through flurries for two days before they found the town. "Found," because the old man was past guiding by then and could only sit his saddle and sing a little, taking deep, gasping breaths to gain the wind to sing again.

Lee found the track to town halfway 'round a mountain to the east of it, questioned Pebble and got weary, closed-eyed nod at this unpromising path, scarcely hoof-beaten, that swung slowly through stands of pine as tall as any Lee had ever seen. These pines—hemlocks, Lee thought—were dark enough green to be black in shadows. Uncomfortable country to travel—so dark, and forested, and narrow on the track, that a man got to wondering just where along his spine a bullet might come knocking to be let in.

They rode that trail safely enough—safely enough for Lee; there was no longer any safety for the old man. He had stopped singing now and Lee had taken him down out of the saddle poles, but had stopped when he saw that the old man was weeping for the shame of it. He had lifted the Cree back up into his saddle, and run a cord around his shrunken middle to the saddle-horn and back to keep him there.

Just so, Lee riding lead and holding a lead rope, the dying old man after, and the wind-broken pack-horse lunging behind—just in that in glorious procession they rode into *Eustache*, and were observed by a considerable crowd of the curious.

Lee saw that he was not cut out to play the Pinkerton, or Secret Agent. All that was lacking was a brass band.

A considerable crowd, and mostly Indians by the look of them. Round-faced, slant-eyed, long black hair done up under caps, and knit hats, scarfs and bright bits of cloth. They were noisy, gabbling at each other, calling out to the old man—his name, Lee supposed, since they seemed to know him. Kids, most of them, a few men holding back a bit, staring. Some rifles among them, but no threatening.

The old man paid no heed, didn't turn his head to look or speak to any of the crowd. Great deal of noise it was getting to be, though; kids at Lee's stirrups, plucking at the grey's tack, seeming to be talking horse-talk with their friends, checking the grey's points as they trotted alongside.

Lee was getting restive for the sight of at

least one white face—didn't know if he was in Red-town, or if this was it, and *Eustache* an Indian settlement. It was not that he was scared of the Indians—they seemed a peaceful enough bunch, none of the edge to them he'd noticed even with trade Sioux coming up around the Rifle River when he was a boy. Woods Indians, he supposed; harsh once, maybe. Tamed now. Crees . . . *Gros Ventres* . . . Those tribes. Chippeways, he'd heard, were still fierce occasionally.

This *Eustache,* or Indian town or whatever, was a long rutted muddy, bordered each side and close by long, low log houses or shanties, looked rather like the places the Irish laborers used to chop and tack up beside the railroad roundhouse in Parker. Except that here there were no wild flowers stuck in pickle jars at the window sills, but rather countless furs and hides nailed and stretched on every rough log wail. Seemed that furs still were a currency in this part of the Canada mountains, anyway. Stuff stunk some, too. Hard to say that trapping was a pleasure to the nose, not in curing time. Lee had done some trapping himself as a boy for pocket money. Mushrat, small beaver, rabbit and so forth. Had bought a Barlow knife that way—Barlow knife and a harmonica. Up here, however, it looked to be an industry. Bear, beaver, lynx, Fisher-cat, marten. Some white weasel, too, even this early.

Smelling the stink of the hides and not a

few other stinks as well—these Indians appeared to have scant notion of out-house and dug latrines—and still leading his noisy procession, Lee saw his first whites, two men standing on a raised walk off to the left in front of some sort of resort—hotel and saloon, it looked like. And mighty poor doings, it seemed—a nasty buck-sawed shack two stories high, with oil-papered windows, split shake roof mended here and there with patches of tarred canvas and tacked tin. Someone had painted a naked woman on the front wall between her two ground-floor windows. Not much of a painting, but he hadn't left anything out, either. Hair between her legs . . . every damn thing.

Big round titties . . . All in sulphurous yellow paint. Not much face, though. That was a circle with a line and two dots. Couldn't be a powerful lot of ladies in Eustache, not and put up with that sort of advertisement. Ladies in Parker would have had that painting scrubbed off the wall in no time flat.

This damn parade had gone on long enough. Lee turned in his saddle and called out, "Any of you people speak English?"

Sudden silence.

The crowd was quiet as be-damned—appeared startled that Lee had the power of speech at all. Lee heard one of the white men laugh, across the street. He cut a look at them. One a short, fat fellow in a knit

sweater, wore an oiled mustache like a bartender's. The second man was taller, dressed
in a dirty brown suit. He had a long forked
beard, and looked to wear a large revolver
under his coat. An armpit holster, perhaps.

"I can speak that."

It was one of the Indian men, a hard-look-
ing article with a Winchester rifle across his
arm, a white man's shirt and trousers on. He
was standing back at the edge of the crowd,
and didn't appear likely to come closer.

"You know this old man?" Pebble was
sitting silent, his head bowed, his veiny
hands knotted on the saddle horn.

The Indian with the Winchester appeared
to stare at Pebble closely, as if Lee might be
talking about another old man—perhaps one
in Montana, or Ottowa. Then he made up his
mind. "I know him." And said what seemed
to be Pebble's Indian name.

"Well, he's sick. Where's his house?"

The crowd was listening to this exchange
with the greatest interest imaginable,
whether they understood the English or not.
Lee heard one of the white men say something. The other one laughed and called to
someone else.

The Indian with the Winchester considered this question as carefully as he had considered the other, the shifted the rifle to his
other arm while he thought. Then, after the
piece was comfortably settled, said, "Up the
hill," and indicated a wretched little track a

77

few yards further along with a movement of his head. "Under big tree." He gestured with his free hand. *"Big* tree."

"Thank you." Most civil damn proceeding yet.

Lee clicked to the grey and led on out at a walk. This time the crowd didn't go with him. Either their curiosity was satisfied, or they thought more noise impolite now that one of them had seriously spoken with him. Indian ways . . . Indian reasons. They stood quiet, even the little children, and watched him lead the old man away.

Several white people and some in-between were on the hotel porch now to see the sight. Two ugly fat women with them, and those certainly breeds. No greetings or questions were called, but they talked among themselves and stared at the old man as Lee lead him past. They were as nasty a bunch as Lee ever recalled seeing, and they were talking English, though not Idaho English. Sounded a little like Scotchmen to Lee, what little he could make out. *"Some arse-hole Yank . . ."* he did hear.

Lee turned up the track, looking back to see the lead was untangled, the paint moving nicely along. The track was steep and shelved with stones. Slick, too, from a recent rain, and what seemed to be an occasional flood of garbage, waste water, and traces of human shit. Bad footing, and the old man wouldn't survive a fall . . .

Just as Lee looked back, old Pebble raised his head a little, and stared at him. Didn't seem to know him at all. The old man's nose was running like a child's. Now, away from the crowd, Lee could hear Pebble breathing. It sounded like a steam boiler cooking up. The old Cree had the pneumonia in his lungs, there was no doubt of it.

There were several miserable shacks along this steep way, but no one came stooping out to watch Lee pass. He felt eyes on him nonetheless from dark low doorways, from shutterless windows and cracks in siding planks. Two dogs came barking, but silenced and danced away when Lee slid the coils of the blacksnake whip from around his neck.

He looked back after he had passed these places, but no-one had come out to stare after him.

The track got steeper so the grey had to hunch his shoulders to the climb, and Lee looked back again to see that the paint was steady, the pack-horse shuffling along behind. When he turned 'round, Lee saw his big tree—a whopper of a hemlock, easily a hundred feet high, trunk thick enough to carve a cabin out of.

There was a hut or shanty just beneath it, half hidden in the great fringed green-black droop of its foliage. The shack looked no better or worse than any Lee had seen along this way. Guiding, then, had not paid the old man much, if he did much of it. The job with

Dowd must have come as a godsend for the old man . . .

As he drew nearer, Lee saw there'd been some sad attempt at prettying the little place. There was calico at a window—blue cloth with yellow flowers printed on it and the small planks of the narrow front door had been white washed.

Pitiful doings.

What had been in the back of Lee's mind now came to the fore. If there was no family to care for the old man, then what? Lee would have to nurse him if he couldn't get some woman and hire it done. A mighty unpleasant thought, wiping the old man's butt for him for the lord only knew how many more days and nights. Didn't seem to Lee he deserved that sort of duty as a long-term thing.

The grey stepped over a trash heap, snorting at the stink, and Lee reined him in before that paltry whitewashed door. Didn't look tall enough for a human to come in and out of.

No use waiting for bad news—might as well call it up.

"Hello the house!"

Silence.

"Hello the damn house! If anybody's home, get on out . . . I have a sick man here!"

Another patch of silence. Lee shifted his butt on the grey, seeing nothing to do but get down and get the old man down, go inside and start nursing. Likely the poor old savage had already crapped his trousers.

A latch clacked then, and the hut door swung slowly open.

A tall, big-nosed Indian boy came out and stood looking up at Lee, then over to the old man. At that glance, Lee saw it was a woman, not a boy. A girl, rather, and mighty plain even for an Indian. White man's trousers, a dirty checkered shirt, and a green Hudson's Bay blanket over her shoulders. Couldn't be more than fifteen or sixteen or so. Skinny, dark as a nigger, and a nose on her like a mould-board plow.

Pleasant eyes, though. Dark and on a slant, like S'ien's.

The girl stood staring at the old man, and put her hands up to cover her mouth. The death was plain to see in him, and must have shocked her.

"Sorry to bring . . ." But she paid Lee no heed, ran to the paint, and began talking to the old man in a rapid rattling way, patting his hands and plucking at the lashing holding him up in the saddle. Granddaughter, likely.

Lee swung down from the grey, ground-tied him, stooped to draw the knife from his right boot, and went to help her unfasten old Pebble. They worked together for a moment, Lee cutting the cord, the girl pulling the loop free of the old man's waist. Then, though she tried to help, Lee shouldered her aside and reached up to take the old man in his arms as he sagged.

The Indian was light as a child, eyes closed, sounding that same snoring, bubbling breath.

The girl danced nervously before them, leading Lee into the shack, talking Indian to the sick man in a reassuring way. The old man seemed to Lee to hear none of it. Got him home too damn late. Should have holed up, warmed and fed him instead of traveling . . .

The inside of the shack was cleaner than the out, but there was no-one else there. Lee had expected—hoped—to see some older woman, fat and strong, ready to take care of the old man. No such luck. Unless someone was away from home, it was the girl and nobody else to nurse old Pebble and ease his dying.

Lee did not expect to find a doctor in such a settlement as this even if the white section gentled-up some, but there might be a shaman or healing woman who'd look in.

He'd have to find a new guide, too. Lee thought of the Indian who'd spoken English, the one with the Winchester. Had looked tough enough, hadn't appeared a fool . . .

Someone had tacked magazine pictures to the sagging walls—white ladies in fine feathers in Philadelphia and New York. Lee laid the old man down on the shack's only excuse for a bed—a rawhide stretcher on a frame, with mouse-chewed furs piled on it. The old man screwed up his toothless face and cried when Lee laid him down, dreaming he was a babe again, maybe, and being set down out of his mother's arms.

The plain girl bent over Pebble, murmuring and cooing at him, tugging and tucking at the furs to make him more comfortable. Lee was somewhat ashamed at the relief he felt to have the Cree off his hands. Doubtless the girl could manage—and there was cash coming to her.

"Name?" Lee said to her, and pointed at her. He pointed to himself. "Lee," he said. "Name, Lee Morgan." She glanced up at him —a plain thing, and no mistake; not wonderfully clean about her person, either; he could smell her smoky scent.

"I know you," she said, talking pretty much like a Christian, but with some of the French in her speech like the old man had. "My father's father went to tell you about the little man."

Then she appeared to have no more interest in him, and went bustling about the little shack in the way all women seemed to have, getting a nearly clean rag out of a basket, dipping it in a rusty bucket of water, and going back to her grandfather to clean his face and hands, making soft noises to him all the while, then to set the rag aside and start undressing him.

Lee made a move to help her, but she took his arm in a thin, strong grip, and pushed it away, so he stood back and watched her tending Pebble, stripping him buck naked, and washing him like a lady washed her dog, chattering softly, murmuring, scrubbing gently here and there, going to the bucket for more water.

"Tell me where you get your water; I'll fetch some."

She paid him no mind, just went on with her business. It appeared to Lee that this girl was good enough of nurse. Good enough to see the old man out, certainly, and that was all that was required. He began to wish a bath for himself—hot, to clear the trail dirt off. Some whiskey, and perhaps a whore, if he could find one not actively poxed and just handsome enough to look at. Seemed to him he'd done his duty, bringing the old man home, seeing him settled in.

"Old fellow did a good job," he said. "Made a damn hard ride. I have some money due him. Suppose I should give it to you . . ." The big-nose girl gave him a glance, and went back to work. She had the old Cree's legs up like an infant's, and was mopping gently between.

Lee dug into his jacket pocket for his purse and took a gold ten-dollar piece out of it. He held it out to her, and she set the old man's leg down, draped the rag neatly over his ankle, turned to Lee and took it in one dark, narrow hand. She was tall, for a girl, but bone thin. Her throat was not much bigger around than his forearm.

She looked at the gold piece as if she hadn't seen many.

"That was for guiding me," Lee said, felt like a fool, dug for another ten and handed it over. "I suppose your grandad never got paid for doing for Mister Dowd. That is for that work."

It took no mind-reader to see the girl had never held twenty dollars in her hand at once her whole life long.

"American dollars," she said.

"Good as any up here."

"Yes." She gave him as long a look as she'd given the money. It made Lee uncomfortable.

"He had it coming. He earned it."

"Yes," she said. "I went to Roman Catholic school with Father Pirenne. *Pere Pirenne,*" she said in French, as if that would help him understand. "I went two years."

Damned if Lee could see what that had to do with the twenty dollars, but he nodded pleasantly. Not surprising she was proud of her schooling—hell, he was fairly proud of his, a sight more than two years, and at a damn fine academy, too.

"O.K.?" she said. "O.K. to give five dollars of this to Father Pirenne?"

"Your grandfather earned it; it's all right with him, it's none of my business."

The Big-nose girl nodded, and went to a splintery shelf to drop the two coins into a small rusty can. There was enough left of the label for Lee to see it had held tomatoes. Girl was some trusting or had decided Lee was too rich to need to steal, to have let him see where she was putting the money.

Time to go. The old Cree had commenced to mutter on the cot, drawing slow, noisy breaths.

"What's your name?" Seemed only courteous.

"Charity," the girl said. At first, Lee thought she was being clever, making fun of the rich white man come to call—must have taken her Indian name away and given her that one.

"Pretty name," Lee said, anxious and more anxious to be gone out of this smelly little hutch. He'd done the proper. "Say," he said, "your grandfather being sick, would you know of a man who could guide for me— maybe out to Lake LaBoarde?"

The Big-nose girl, Miss Charity, stood staring at him as if he'd suddenly started talking Swedish (it was a habit these woods Indians seemed to have when asked any question at all). She looked at Lee for a fair amount of time, then shook her head up and down—"no."

"There's an Indian—fellow with a Winchester rifle—looks handy enough . . ."

A swift look of contempt on the girl's face. "Simon Fat-tongue," she said. "He is a thief."

Unfortunate news. Still, there was not much for a thief to steal out in the deep woods, and the fellow'd looked handy—maybe hard enough to be some help . . .

"He tells all secrets," the girl nodded, as if that clinched it. And maybe it did. Had to find some sort of guide, though—that, or wander the mountains following some fool's map. Something to think about and no use thinking about it here. A wash-tub full of hot water was calling. A wet tub, a wet glass, a wet cunt all calling loud and clear. And some word to get, too, on this "White Chief Surrey," and Jacques Forge.

"Do you need any help from me?" Catherine Dowd would have approved the question.

"No," she said. "I do not." It was a shame about that nose; it surely spoiled her looks.

Lee went over to the cot and bent to the old man. "Pebble," he said, down close to the old man's ear. "Do you hear me?" and was slightly surprised when the old man opened his eyes and regarded Lee with that steady, wise gaze that dogs and babies occasionally employed.

"Morgan," the old man said, in a voice out of water. Then he said, "Where have you brought me?"

"To your home, old man—with my thanks for your courage and skill in coming down to get me." Lee patted the old man's arm and straightened up to go, but the Indian made a feeble clutch at him and he paused, then bent to hear what the Cree had to say. The old man muttered softly into Lee's ear, then cleared his throat and spoke more clearly. "You foolish on slide on mountain. Funny. Make my belly shake to see . . ."

"Glad you enjoyed it," Lee said, and patted the old man's arm again. "I thought you might have taken that trail a-purpose, you old son-of-a-bitch!"

He stood straight, liking the old man a good deal, and sad to see him dying. "I'll be going on," he said to the girl. "Is there a clean place to stay the night in town?"

"Rich whites stay in Albert's," she said, and stood staring at Lee as if expecting some fabulous reply.

"Thank you. Well—I'll be going, then. Hope he'll be some better in the morning. . ."

The Big-nose girl had nothing to say to that, so Lee put his hat on and turned and left, ducking deep to clear the door-top.

There was some slight trash on the packy that belonged to the old man, but damned if Lee felt like popping the pack and dumping it here to paw through it. Hell, twenty dollars gold would more than cover an old fry-pan, coffee pot with a leak to it, a second blanket (with fleas for sure) and a buffalo robe seen better days. He'd stopped long enough.

He climbed up on the grey, reined it 'round, and was surprised to see the Big-nose girl watching from her doorway. He lifted his hat to her as if she'd been a lady.

Then he spurred down-trail, the blower of a pack-horse clattering behind. A neat rain came out of the grey sky, as if to gust him on his way.

CHAPTER FOUR

Eustache turned out to be a long road, curving slowly around the foot of a mountain. Indian town had only been Indian town—there was a white section, neater, the outsides of the cabins and log shacks whitewashed. And a great deal of traffic on the road—a swarm of people afoot (a novelty to Lee, though on reflection he could see that a canoe or good pair of boots might do a man very well in river country, in thick forest, and no horse required) and a fair trundling of freight wagons, log-skidders, barrows, burthens and teams.

But the white faces showed as little joy as had the red. It was a poor settlement, for all its business in the street (called *Main*, of course). And it seemed to Lee, from the voices he heard, that the French were fading out and the English-speakers moving in. English voices, or at least Canadian-Scotch voices, everywhere overpowered and out-shouted the French. A lot of rifles—not so many revolvers—in people's hands, or strapped across their backs. Hunting knives and rifles . . . Only a few revolver butts at belts, in holsters.

Men and women, few of the women all-the-way white, stared at Lee as he rode by, obviously recognizing an American. One man, a fat fellow in a yellow canvas jacket, spit off a boardwalk as Lee passed. Might not have meant an insult by it. Might have been carelessness.

The rain came and went as Lee rode the town—didn't appear to be much to the place off this broad, muddy, wheel-trenched street. Stores, cabins, saloons, lean-to shacks, ware-houses, restaurants (these seeming pretty vil-lainous, despite some fancy French names painted on their sign-boards), harness-makers, eyeglass sellers, dentists—all the crowd of them lining this single long street. Women hanging out their washing and slapping their kids right next to some vicious resort featuring a line of drunks pissing off a porch while a squaw (even drunker) hoisted her skirt and squatted to match them.

A hard town, and a poor one. Not one of the businesses looked prosperous, not even the saloons. Still, there was an air of . . . ex-pectation. Lee had seen it once or twice elsewhere. A poor, rough town, on the edge of wilderness. Everyone waiting for the bonanza, whatever that might be. Furs? Lee thought not. Lumber? Maybe. Mining? Cattle?

Something. These people were sure of something; they just weren't sure what.

The rain was coming down steadily now, light, constant, chill drizzle. The sky over the bulk of the mountain above was grey as a dirty shirt—would have looked to threaten snow, if it had covered Idaho. Lee suspected that it threatened snow in Canada just as surely.

He was anxious, and the grey was anxious, and the wind-popped packy was anxious to find someplace warm and dry. Lee asked a man who looked like an English-speaker about Albert's. Fellow spoke French at Lee for some time, then turned and walked away. Had been wearing a fine wolf parka, though —might be handier in thick forest than Lee's long, heavy buffalo coat which was about as heavy as his sleeping robe.

Lee asked two other people. One, a pleasant looking white woman with a market basket, was new in town, visiting her son, and didn't know of the place. The other was a teamster, who looked sober as a parson as Lee approached him, and turned out to be dead drunk, though sitting upright on his dray, flourishing his whip and cursing like the Jehu of Jehus. Could curse, but couldn't speak, he was that drunk.

Leaving the fellow cursing in the middle of the street, Lee kicked the weary grey into a trot splashing and squelching through the mud and reached up to strike the soaked brim of his Stetson clear of water; the thing was drooping down like a cut flower and draining rain down Lee's jacket collar. Having made this adjustment, Lee looked out across Main Street (now a waste of water wet as any lake) and saw a neat sign in black and yellow—*ALBERT'S*, fronting a handsome whitewashed house two stories high. This looked to be a prime lodging, and was the most welcome sight Lee had seen in some time.

He was not disappointed.

There was, in turned out, no Albert, but there was a Mister Gruen, a tall, stately old sissy in a neat set of trousers (pale grey) and a black swallow-tail coat.

Mister Gruen was not daunted by Lee's trail dirt or two weeks' worth of beard. Was happy to see him, in fact, because two mineral men from Toronto had just checked out and left him a vacancy—a small room behind the house, over the back porch. It was two dollars a night (room and partial board— Mister Gruen's celebrated sour-dough flap-jack breakfast). A little steep, Lee thought, but worth it.

Mister Gruen helped him unsaddle the

grey and take off the horse-pack, chatting all the while about the hardships of life on the Canadian frontier, particularly the hardships of dealing with the French who thought they knew everything about everything, and particularly about cooking.

That done, Mister Gruen led Lee to the bath-house, drew him a steaming tub—"I fire this awful boiler myself, morning and evening. It's one of the trials of inn-keeping" —and stayed for a moment to see that Lee had the soap he required, and that the water was not too hot. Then, with a murmured "You're certainly a well-set-up young fellow," and he strolled out and left Lee in peace and contentment, parboiling the trail muck off in a haze of soap-smell and steam.

He bathed and soaked for more than half an hour, then climbed out of the tub, toweled dry except for his face, dug his razor out of his war-bag, lathered up, and shaved. Then clean socks; a fresh long-john shirt (his last outerwear one was still with old Pebble) a clean pair of Levi tent-cloth trousers; his buckskin jacket—worn and not warm enough for this weather—and he was ready to walk out on the town, after buckling on the Colt's and slipping his knife down into his right boot.

There was a stop to be made beforehand, however, and Lee sat enthroned upon Mister Gruen's back-yard crapper (a three-holer) and read from the Sear's and Roebuck catalogue while listening to the last few skirmishes of rain tapping on the out-house tin.

"Where to go for a jolly time?" had been the question he then had for Mister Gruen, finding that gent at work in his kitchen. There'd been another boarder there as well sitting at the deal table, puffing on a long-stem pipe. A solid built old man with a bushy beard just run to salt, and one wise and one wandering eye. McReedy, he called himself, and spoke with the same Scotch accent Lee had heard in the streets and from Mister Gruen. They said "*aboot*" instead of about, and spoke a little more formally than Americans might.

"A jolly time?" the old man said, butting in without apology. "Would you be wanting a smooth time, now? Or rougher?"

"Now, Bob . . ." said Mister Gruen.

"I'm ashamed to say . . . rougher," Lee said, and the other two laughed.

"There's the Fine Canteen, in Skin-town," the old man said.

"God," said Mister Gruen. "Don't send the boy there!"

"Then there's Barney Barkley's place . . ."

"Even worse," said Mister Gruen. "The two nastiest joints in the town."

"Boy said 'Rougher.' "

"Which is closer?" Lee said, shaking his head at Mister Gruen, who was indicating in dumb show that he was making roast beef sandwiches, and asking if Lee wanted one.

"Barney's," the old man said, and paused to relight his pipe. "You would be a tough customer, wouldn't you?" (Puff, puff.)

Lee thought about it for a moment, then smiled and said that he supposed that he was.

"In that case," McReedy said, "you might enjoy Barney's. You might also get into trouble there."

"The two often go together, I've found," Lee said. And McReedy laughed, and turned to Mister Gruen at the kitchen counter. "A philosophical Yankee—what next?"

Barney Barkley's didn't look too fierce, not from the outside. The rain had stopped but a cold wind was hauling in the night to replace it. Lee had followed directions down two blocks of sagging boardwalk and across Main Street in knee-deep mud to arrive at the place.

Barney's was a cluster of split-log cabins all, like most of the white section's buildings, whitewashed. Some music was leaking out of a half shuttered window, and Lee could see the bouncing shadows of dancers against a section of lamplit wall inside.

Inviting enough, though the plank sign outside featured a hanged man holding another sign in his hands.

"BARNEY'S."

Lee climbed the boardwalk steps, scraped

some of the mud off his boots on a splintered stoop, pushed open the door, and walked in.

This was the dancing room, and no-one paid him a bit of heed.

An accordian and a fiddle were being worked in a far corner—worked about as well as Lee had ever heard—and the puncheon floor of the small cabin was being pounded like a drum by the boots and moccasins of a dozen big men and an equal number of Indian women considerably shorter but just as wide. Likely about as strong, too, Lee thought, seeing one of them, a fat and greasy creature with hams like a four-year steer, lift her partner up in the dance (and him not small and light as a daisy) and twirl him as if he were a debutante girl at a Boston cotillion.

The noise was terrific and continuous, and the stink was the same—bear oil, neat's foot oil, Macassar oil, sweat and still more sweat, stale beer and raw whiskey (a touch of vomit, too), and over all the stench of curing hides and rain-soaked wool.

Most of the dancers were too busy to notice him, but Lee saw one squaw, broad in the beam as San Franciso smack, giving him the eye as she spun. The fellow spinning her looked French—dark as she was, round as a barrel, hands like baseball catcher's mitts. For so big a woman, the Indian danced light as a gas balloon, fairly tripping back and forth in her fringed moccasins, prancing here and there, out-wrestling her partner where need be. Fellow kept grappling at her breasts, but she elbowed him away every time, and used these occasions to roll a roguish eye in Lee's direction.

A down whore, and charming in her way, Lee thought her. Likely a terror as so many Indians were in her cups, but a thunderous ride and good company, if an eye was kept on her knife-hand . . .

Lee blew her a kiss for keepers, then turned and waded his way to the inside door to find the bar.

The bar-room was larger than the dance-hall, and less crowded—a long, narrow two-log-length space with the plank ceiling no more than a foot or so over a man's head as he walked. The bar was a stretch of planed timber braced on saw horses, the bottles and kegs ranked along the log wall behind.

Two bartenders, both small men with fine mustaches, were busy serving out the gut and suds. The room wasn't crowded—not surprising, since there was no place to sit down, no tables, no chairs, not even benches. The bar *was* crowded, with a quiet crowd of hard drinkers, or Lee had never seen one. Same gopher-looking bunch as dancing, he thought, likely some hard-cases amongst them . . .

Two men looked 'round as Lee walked to the bar, then went back to minding their drinks and their business.

"What'll it be?" The bartender was wearing a clean shirt, as near as Lee could tell in the lamplight. Must be a particular fellow —or it be Wednesday and wash-day.

"Double whiskey."

"House or the Bay's?" By which Lee supposed he meant a choice of Hudson's Bay Company liquor.

"House," he said, and the bartender smiled, reached behind him (without looking), pulled a grimy looking bottle out of the row on the wall shelf, then brought it around, thumbed it open, and produced a big chip-rimmed glass mug to pour into.

"I can see you're a sport," the bartender said, and slid the mug over to him.

"Just curious," Lee said, and drank the stuff down.

"Well, Yank," the bartender said, watching Lee's face. "And is your curiosity satisfied?"

"I've had worse," Lee said—and he had, but not much worse.

"Another?" A noisy three or four were stomping into the place for the dancing.

"Once was fair," Lee said, "and once was enough. I'll try the other."

The bartender nodded. Lee saw that his shirt was clean, but his neck was dirty. "You're a sensible fella," he said, and reached behind him for a different bottle, without looking. "The Bay makes decent drink."

He might have said more, but Lee didn't hear it—one of the men in from the dancing had stepped up to the bar beside him, shouldered Lee roughly, not gotten enough room, then, half turning, put out an arm like a hickory branch, planted his hand on Lee's chest, and shoved him a yard down the bar.

Lee's mug went to the sawdust and he tripped going back and had to catch himself on the bar edge. Felt a fool, not being ready for it and having heard them come in noisy.

The man who'd pushed him didn't even look 'round. The bartender glanced at Lee, amused. It had been a considerable shove. Hard to let it pass. The bully's back was wide as a door. He wore a brown wool shirt, and had clusters of hair as golden as a girl's at the back of his head. Was a couple of inches taller than Lee.

Lee took a breath, and decided to let it pass. The fellow was big, and with friends, and it wasn't enough to be a killing matter. Not in a strange country.

The noise at the bar had increased with these men coming into it. The music and dancing in the room next door sounded louder now, too.

Lee stepped back up to the bar, well away from the big man with the yellow hair, and signaled the barkeep for his whiskey. The barman came down smiling, and slid a fresh mug across. This one had no chips out of the rim, and Lee counted himself lucky.

"Very reasonable of you, Yank," the bartender said, and nodded in the direction of the big man's back. "Very reasonable."

No sooner were the words said, than—perhaps joined by another friend, perhaps to make mischief—the big man half turned, took a long step down the bar, and put his shoulder hard into Lee's. The whiskey was jolted out of the mug, splashing down Lee's long-john shirt and he saw, over the blond man's massive shoulder, the profile of his face, watching. The man, who by his pretty hair might have been expected handsome, was a dish-face thing, with a swollen jaw and brows. Blue eyes bulging as shallow as painted china.

"Make more room, Yankee," he said to Lee. Someone had hit the fellow in his throat once, and spoiled it. His voice was broken and had a squeak to it.

"Yes, I will," Lee said to that half-turned face—and swung full-armed overhand and hit the fellow on his left ear with the edge of the glass mug. The blow made a sharp *chunk* sound as it struck.

"Shit!" the bartender said, and jumped back against the wall. And Lee stepped back, too, a long fast step as the big man turned like a swinging door and reached out for Lee with both hands. He wore no revolver. Had a sheath-knife on his hip.

Lee stepped back again, and when the blond man leaned forward, reaching, his eyes showing no particular emotion, nothing of pain or anger, Lee lunged suddenly in, swung the mug overhand again, and hit the man down across the bridge of his nose. The bone in it cracked with a small delicate snapping sound, and blood came out, just a little.

The blond man shook his head as if he recognized that pain, and very quickly got his hand onto his knife hilt, drew the weapon, and swung it very hard at Lee's right side. Lee got his arm down in time to block the stab—down, but not strongly enough; the dish-faced man was powerful as a horse. His wrist hit Lee's arm and knocked it back into him with the knife coming along in that massive clenched fist.

Lee twisted left, felt the trickling as the blade slid and sliced so quickly across some skin of his belly—kept turning as fast as he could, smashed the mug against the bar-planks and twisted back to slam the handle and a handful of splintered glass into the big man's face.

It struck and stuck there, driven into the bone of the man's cheek and jaw, and Lee had to tear it away and jump back for his life as the big man swung his knife again, crowding him, bulling him back. The blood was running like rain water all over the blond man's face.

He didn't seem to mind it.

Lee was standing out in the middle of the floor glad of the room and the man came loping after him like an ape. Lee still had a piece of the mug handle in his hand, and he dropped it, stooped, and drew the double-edged dagger from his right boot. Blond fellow didn't hesitate—came right in, shaking his head, spattering blood.

Lee danced backward, trying to keep away —saw roaring bearded faces along the bar. Couldn't hear any noise, though. Just like a dream. He wished to God he could use his pistol on this man without these people stringing him up.

The big man was following fast . . . but it seemed to Lee now that it was all moving slowly, both the big man and he, moving as if they were both dreaming about this fight . . .

The man came swinging, and Lee felt the snag as the fellow's blade caught the cloth of his shirt. Son of a bitch was ruining the only clean shirt Lee had to his name!

Saw a woman watching. Fat, sweaty round Indian face.

The big man came again—rushing in, blank-eyed, swinging that mighty arm. The hunting knife.

Lee ducked inside the swing and jumped away, felt the impact of the boot soles on the puncheon floor as he leaped. Not many more of those in him before the fellow caught him fairly and they wrestled and chopped, looking for a final stab into the gut. Lee felt he couldn't be badly hurt—couldn't afford it, somehow, win or lose.

He decided to kill this big, hurrying man.

When the blond man rushed again, Lee turned and ran halfway down the length of the room—heard the howling, the noise of the watchers seeing a finish, then spun as the dish-faced man came galloping, drew back his knife-hand underarm—then shoveled the double-edged blade up from under and out. The border toss, Lee's heard it called. Not much power to the throw, compared to an overhand pitch. Not enough power for a throw into the chest.

The needle point of the dagger took the blond man neatly under his great chin and slid on in as if sheathed, the leather-wrapped handle jutting out like some enormous stick-pin thrust out of his throat.

The man kept taking swift, pounding strides, his shallow eyes fixed on Lee as they had been since the fight began. He seemed not to realize what had happened for several seconds, and Lee backed away as if from death coming in woodsman's boots.

There was not a sound in the bar room now except for Lee's harsh breathing, his boot-steps, the echoing strides of the man with the knife in his throat.

It was no air to breathe that slowed and

stopped him. Then the dish-faced man stood puzzled for a few seconds, trying to find a breath. He dropped his knife onto the floor in his confusion, and reached up with both hands to touch at the dagger handle, to tug at it gently.

Then the china blue eyes showed something, and he grasped the dagger handle and pulled at it, but not too strongly. Some of the flat, gleaming blade slid out of his throat a little, greasy with blood, and letting more blood out. The big man, his golden curly hair all dank and dark with sweat, sank to his knees in the sawdust, still fingering at the dagger's handle, but not gripping it with full strength, not tearing it out of him.

The big man's face was turning darker in the lamp light. He lay down on his side then, turned to his back, his chest heaving as he tried to breathe. His china blue eyes had rolled up and back into his head. Only the whites showed now.

Slowly . . . slowly . . . the heavy boots began to lift and fall, kicking left, then right, the boot-heels drumming a slow tattoo on the puncheon floor. The man's tongue was out of his mouth now like a blue snake's head, seeking air.

Lee felt as tired as he could remember feeling. Felt as if he must get to sleep or would die of being so tired. He forced himself to the effort of walking to the dying man, forced himself to the effort of bending over him, and grunted with effort as he pulled the dagger free, gripped the strangling man by his fine hair, and cut his damaged throat from one ear to the other.

Stood up from that, to a room of silence.

The dancing had stopped in the other room; the music had stopped. No-one was even talking. Lee looked around at them, something dismayed by the silence. Certainly they had seen that bully or other bullies fight. Certainly had seen some of those hard-cases killed. Why such silence then? He'd cut the man's throat as a favor and any sensible man would have seen it so.

"Don't be so damn quiet," he said to them. "It was only a fight and he got the worst of it." And he found his Stetson, picked it up, and put it on.

"That's right," a woman said, and stood by the dance-hall door, looking at him. It was the fat whore who'd eyed him in the dance-hall. Lee saw her round, beaming, dark, dirt-smudged face more clearly than any other in the place. It may have been the flickering, smoky lamplight, it may have only been that hers was the best face to see. The other people were looking at him with an odd look, every one of them. They wouldn't meet his eyes—it was like looking into the faces of cattle or horses.

Only the fat Indian woman looked straight at him.

"Is there any sort of law here?" Lee said.

None of them said a word. Two men slid out the dance-hall door, and went. Others were standing staring down at the dead man. The dish-faced man lay in a tremendous spreading pool of blood black as tar, reflecting the bar-room's lights. The big man looked shrunken . . . his pretty hair would be soaked, glued into the puddle of blood under the back of his head. Wouldn't have imagined anything like this could have happened to him just coming into a favorite ken for a drink . . . have a shove at a cowboy Yank . . .

And look what happened.

Shrunken and shorter, lighter in weight, narrower in the shoulder . . . now that he was dead.

"I suppose I look smaller now . . . They always looked smaller to me." His father, lying on that cook-shack floor, looking up at him. With not much left to say and not much time to say it.

Lee felt tired of the way they were looking at him. "I asked you people a question. There some law in this town should know about this?"

The bartender—man with the clean shirt—called across the room to him as some more men slid out the dance-hall door, not wanting any part of more trouble, apparently—not wanting to see any more, either, "There's a Mountie post in town, Yank. One riding officer. He's gone off to catch a thief."

108

That was good news, Lee supposed. He'd heard the Mounted Police were nasty customers, snotty, and pleased to use steel handcuffs on people when they arrested them. Couldn't see himself bound in steel handcuffs. And wouldn't care to have to kill a Canadian policeman about it.

"You come here," the fat Indian woman said. She came to him and put her broad brown hand gently on his arm, as if he were a restive horse, a stallion who had just injured someone.

"You come here with me, Pretty-boots," the Indian woman said, and gripped his arm tighter and began to lead him away, back through the door into the dance-hall whre the two musicians and a few others stood against the wall, drinking mugs of beer and watching Lee and the whore walk through. A difference, Lee thought, between these people and Americans. In such a harsh town in the States, in such a circumstance, the musicians would already be back to playing, the little room roaring, jumping, pounding under the dancers' feet.

A solemn bunch, up here. Came, no doubt, from not having kicked the British out.

She led him out a back door, and down a log walled corridor just wide enough to pass, his shoulders brushing as they walked. The Indian woman was in front of him, shorter than she had seemed out in the saloon. Stocky work-horse haunches on her . . . that pigeon-toed walk all Indians seemed to have. She smelled of beer and sweat and campfires.

Wonderful hair, though, black and gleaming as oil-tar. The woman wore it twisted into a knot at the back of her head. Looked like S'ien's, was the truth of the matter. Lee supposed there was something to the Indians being some sort of Orientals after all. That rich, shining black hair was very like S'ien's.

The woman came to a rough plank door and pushed it open. Lee followed her inside not concerned some badger might be there, seeking his purse. If there was such a crimp in prey at Barney Barkley's and he troubled Lee, then so much the worse for him.

The crib was empty and no larger than a coal bin.

The pitch pine walls had been whitewashed, though, and decorated with pictures of white ladies from the *roto gravures*—handsome women with curls at their foreheads, stepping in and out of carriages in some Eastern cities, always with tall men, mustachioed and in silk high hats standing at their elbows to support them. Very like the pictures that old Pebble's granddaughter had tacked up in her shanty.

Lee supposed that the Indian women, seeing the white men had beaten their men at every point, and seeing that white ladies nevertheless ruled those same conquerors, sought in these pictures from the East some notion of what white women's secret power might be.

"Put away?"

The fat whore stood looking up at him, something reticent, an inquiring expression on her face.

"Put away . . . ?"

Lee had no idea what she was talking about.

"Put *what* the hell away?"

The woman pointed down to his right hand and Lee saw that he still gripped the dagger, the broad blade bared, smeared with reddish black in a thick way, as if he had been slicing a chocolate cake with it. His fist was still clenched around the weapon as if it had not yet received any news of victory, any permit for ease.

Lee felt a fool, knowing why the people had stared so, been so odd in dealing with him after the fight. He smiled at the woman to reassure her, then unclenched his fist— or tried to—that grip was reluctant to relax— but did unclench it, wiped the knife, before he thought, on his only clean trousers, and stooped to slide the blade into the sheath in his right boot.

Folks must have thought he'd run mad, lounging around with the knife out in that fashion, and the fight over and done with.

"I forgot," he said to the whore, and

wondered if they'd gotten that bully up off the floor and out of the place. Damned if he wanted to go out and see the fellow still lying there. There was no reason to be seeing that again. Over and done with, and that was that. He took off his jacket, hung it on one of a row of nails beside the door, unbuckled his gun-belt and hung that up as well.

The woman, some easier now, apparently —and sturdy of her, after all, to have brought him back, and him with that knife still fisted —now came up to cuddle in a pleasant whorish way, making him familiar of her softness and heat. She smelled of sweat and wood smoke. Pleasant . . . a pleasant smell.

Nothing in the crib by way of furniture except for cot and a nailed-up table with a water basin and kerosene lamp on it.

"You good fighter," the woman said. She was unbuttoning him, shirt and trousers, as smoothly as any mother might her child's.

"Don't talk about that," Lee said. "I don't need to hear about that."

She smiled and nodded, and said, "You deal horses? You buy—you sell horses?" She knelt before him easily, for all her flash, and tugged his trousers down. "You sit."

Lee sat down on her bed, feeling tired out, and she pulled off his boots, then took off his socks, then slid his trousers off. "I do sell horses," Lee said. "I raise them."

"So," the Indian woman said. "Strong horses? Fast horses?" She reached up and Lee raised his buttocks so she could pull his underpants down.

"Strong *and* fast. The best."

The fat woman smiled and shook her head. She put both plump hands on him and began to knead and stroke his cock. "Not so," she said. *"Nez Perce* make horses strong and fast. White mens do not."

"My father had a stallion from them," Lee said.

"You have a nice thing," the Indian woman said, stroking gently at him. She squeezed it as it stood swollen in her hands. Knelt up a little, and kissed the tip of it—a wet, affectionate, smacking kiss. She smiled up at Lee. "Not so big, though, as stallion has!" and giggled.

"Take your clothes off," Lee said, "and get up on the bed."

She let go of him, and stood up with a grunt, her round, dark face shining in the lamp light. Held out her hand.

"Two dollar," she said.

Lee sat up, reached down his jacket, dug into a pocket for his purse, took out five dollars and handed the money to her.

She looked down at it without any expression, though Lee doubted she usually received so much and more than she'd asked, then tucked up her flower print calico and stuffed the cash down into the top of her black cotton stocking. A folded straight razor was lying under a frilled garter on the fat, muscular thigh of her other leg.

Then she let her hem fall, and commenced to unbutton the dress, opened it down the front, and took it off.

Except for her stockings and her garter, she was stark naked. Dark, dark brown all over—her skin the color of wet clay-dirt, and smooth as panelled wood. She was round and fat and powerful looking as a skinned bear, with broad dark brown settings for her nipples—small breasts, plump with fat, big broad belly and hips, and flanks like a pony's. Her cunt was shaved quite clean of hair—to keep off lice and such, Lee supposed —and was left as small and simple as a child's. Dimpled and closed up tight. No sign of pink meat showing.

She smiled under Lee's gaze as if she were Lillian Russell herself, stripped for Brady or the Commodore, and turned slowly 'round to show her ass—round brown melons shining in the lamp light. Her back looked narrow above those rounds, but wasn't; she had a back as broad as a man's, and likely as strong. Her backbone was sunk in fat and muscle.

She looked back over her shoulder at him, smiling with pleasure and pride at the display of herself—her simple, fat, sturdy body. It made Lee feel tender toward her.

"Come here," he said, and when she came to stand before him at the cot, put his hands on her naked hips, leaned forward, kissed her brown belly, and blew gently into her belly button, making a soft farting sound.

She gave a little jump, as if startled, then threw back her head and laughed like a man, imitated the same sound with her lips, and laughed some more.

Lee supposed people in the place must think something odd, to hear child's play through the walls of a whore's crib.

"What's your name?" he said to the fat woman smiling down at him.

"Mary."

"Your real name . . . your Indian name."

But she shook her head, and wouldn't tell it. It was her secret.

Lee reached out and stroked her small, fat mound . . . slid a finger up the crease . . . probed her with it, gently, and found her hole—narrow, tight, slippery with her oils.

"Good," she said, and climbed up onto his lap, her strong, fat legs astraddle. She hiked herself up higher, holding his cock like a handle to steady herself, raised her loins, and then carefully fitted him into her . . . just the head of his cock wedging into the small heat and slickness.

"O.K.?" she said and sat down on him a little deeper.

"O.K." Lee said, shrugged off his opened shirt so as to feel her fully against him, put his arms around her—felt all her weight and strength and softness—hugged her hard, and slowly began to drive his cock up into her.

She murmured against his throat and he felt her tense as he held her. Then she eased and opened, and he slid up into her all the way. There were things at play within her—shifting, wet, hot passages gripping him as hard as ever he'd gripped his knife. He felt wet at the hairs of his crotch; she was running liquid down him as they moved, as he thrust up and into her. She moved on him as if she were riding a horse in the Eastern style, posting.

She smelled of fish now, as the oil came out of her cunt, that smell so much richer than any that came from the body of a man. A rich fish stink to grow a baby in.

In his enjoyment, Lee still felt what a foolish thing it was to pay a woman to pretend at baby making only so the man could work his cock to sneeze and then go off well satisfied.

The whore clung to him sturdily now, thrusting herself up and down his pole, working hard enough so that Lee thought she might be getting pleasure from it. He took her shoulders and pushed her back a little so that he could see her face—round, flushed, contorted with effort. Her eyes were squinted almost shut.

They made wet sounds where they joined. The fat woman began to grunt each time she sat down fully on him, each time his cock went up her all the way. She grunted, and Lee felt her strong fingers gripping at his shoulders, squeezing and pinching at him.

He slid his hands down to her ass, took each large buttock in a grip, and commenced to help her where she wished to go—lifting her high, almost off him, then hauling her down onto it again. All the way. Her long black hair was coming down, streaming over her shoulders.

She muttered something to him in Indian and leaned forward to bite at the side of his neck. That bite—nervous, tentative, delicate —as if she were speaking to him in a manner more personal than cries, began to force from Lee a sweetness that he could no longer hold. He hugged her to him as if he loved her, as if he knew her better than something bought. They hugged each other like friends in pursuit of some great prize. They galloped together, her round face furious with concentration, shiny with sweat, her plump, small breasts shaking as she rode.

Lee felt the jissom rising from his stones, and the fat woman felt the change in him as it happened. She crowed, and bounced on him like an India-rubber ball, all sweaty and beaming, and her cunt held him, and wrung him, and worked the cum out of him in long, long spurts.

It felt as if he'd turned to honey and was

melting out.

"Ooooh . . ." she said, and pursed her lips in a little "O." "*Oooooohh* . . ." Lee felt her cunt contract around him, clenching, soaked and soft.

They stopped moving slowly, together, much as Lee had seen a railroad locomotive wheel slowly, slowly turn to a stop. The high wheel, the drive-shafts . . . the pistons moving slowly to a stop.

She lay against him, lay in his arms like a wife, her face buried in his shoulder, her fat, round belly warm against his.

Lee leaned back against the rough blank wall, holding her as she held him. To have made a down whore come was no small thing and he was proud of it.

Of course, to have made a blood-sick man a lover was no small thing either.

They sat together for a little while, then Lee felt her cunt slowly contracting, slowly recovering its privacy as his wet, limp cock slid out of her into cool air.

She sat back in his arms and looked at him. There'd been a wet sound as their sweaty skins had parted.

"Good fight. Good fuck," she said, and smiled at him.

Lee grieved his last for the slain bully, seeing that this woman had good sense. He leaned forward and kissed the whore on her lips. She stared, astonished at his doing such a thing, and Lee gently eased her off his lap, stood up, and gathered his clothes.

It was time to walk back to Albert's through the cold night air.

Time for a long, sweet sleep.

CHAPTER FIVE

"Well, you've certainly blotted *your* copy-book, Mister Morgan." Mister Gruen had waited until his other guests had left the breakfast table—two fur buyers from Victoria, a lumber man, and old McReedy—before giving Lee a small piece of his mind. Which was all right with Lee—he had some questions to ask the inn-keeper.

"I don't know," Mister Gruen said, pouring Lee a second cup of coffee, "I don't know the state of the law down in your country, but I can assure you that the Mounted Police take a *very* dim view of killings up here! Not that the fellow you bumped was an exemplary citizen—no one thinks that . . ."

He put the coffee pot down and sat down himself. It had been a rather quiet breakfast; McReedy and the others had had nothing much to say, had kept their faces to their plates for the most part.

"The constable here," Gruen said, "providentially out of town now, is a sergeant named Ferguson. An extremely severe young man who takes no nonsense, I assure you." Gruen took a cold biscuit from the bread plate, and buttered it. "It would be very wise —*very* wise of you, to scoot back over the border without delay. Ferguson might not . . ."

"Have you heard of a man named Surrey?" Lee said. "And a man named Jacques Forge?"

"Did you hear a word that I said?"

"Certainly did," Lee said, "and I appreciate it. Good advice and I'll certainly follow it just as quick as I can. A fellow named Surrey? Jacques Forge?"

Mister Gruen sat nibbling at his biscuit, regarding Lee with some discouragement.

"Is this about the Dowd affair? Is this about that?"

"You bet."

Mister Gruen finished his biscuit. "Don't let anybody tell you that beaten biscuits are superior. It's nonsense. Simply nonsense."

Lee nodded though he didn't entirely agree. He'd had beaten biscuits and they definitely had the edge over straight baked.

"Mister Dowd," Gruen said, "attempted the life of Lord Surrey, and in the ensuing struggle was wounded and died." He sat back in his chair, fixing Lee with a school-master's look. "That was the tale that Lord Surrey told; that was the tale that Surrey's man, Robins, told. Dowd—whose reputation in the Provinces was not of the best—was dead, and had no story to tell. As to Forge, the man had an evil reputation, lives deep in the mountains, and as far as I know, has never even been seen in *Eustache* or near it."

"Dowd's guide came down to get me," Lee said. "Mister Dowd was a good friend; the guide said he was murdered with no chance at all."

"An Indian guide?"

"That's right," Lee said.

"Good lord, young man—Indians have their own notion of fact. Surely you know that—you're a westerner!"

"It sounded true to me."

Mister Gruen got up from the table and began collecting the dishes to wash. "I've never heard of such foolishness—not, I suppose, that it's any of my business. I *do* feel responsible for old McReedy's advisory to you on local entertainment. I notice he had the grace to keep his mouth shut this morning!"

"Tell me about this Lord Surrey," Lee said. "Is he a real English lord or posing?"

"Oh, the genuine article, I can assure you of that," Gruen said from the sink. "And if you think that doesn't mean something in this country, young man, you have another think coming! Surrey is a handsome boy, very, very rich—and *very* well connected, in the mother country of course, and in Ottawa."

Lee finished his coffee. Well into the morning. Time to get moving. "And what's such a precious article doing out here?"

"The 'precious article' is out here representing his family—their investments, in any case. His father is the Duke of Morne, if that means anything to you. The boy is an Earl."

"They might be a greedy bunch," Lee said, and Gruen laughed, drying a plate with a small striped towel. "Well," he said, "I suppose that they are and have been for some centuries. Doesn't mean the boy murdered Mister Dowd." He picked up another plate.

"How in hell you people put up with those English aristrocrats, I'll never understand. We kicked their butts out long ago!"

Gruen turned from the sink, towel in one hand, wet cup in the other.

"Did you really? I understand that you people are very ready to welcome investments from those 'English aristocrats.' And I would add that when we meet such a person, whatever we might think of the individual we *are* impressed by the history they represent. Something Americans would not understand." Turned back to his sink, looking mighty stiff, and said, with his back turned,

"You'd be very wise, Mister Morgan, to concern yourself with constable Ferguson and leave Lord Surrey to his explorations."

"I meant no offense, Mister Gruen," Lee said, getting up from the table. "When in Rome . . ."

"Just so," Gruen said, from the sink.

"Quite right about those biscuits, too," Lee said. "Doubt I've ever had better."

"It's the dough," Mister Gruen said, and hung up his dish towel. "It's all in the dough. Most people knead their dough to death and their biscuits taste it."

"If you'll tote up the bill," Lee said, "I'll be paying and on my way."

"Oh," said Mister Gruen, holding out his hand to shake, "bed and breakfast'll run you the two dollars—unless you're strapped." He looked some concerned. "If you're caught short, seeing that you're a guest in the country, and in some difficulty—and seeing that it was in my kitchen that fool McReedy gave you ill advice—I'll knock that down to a dollar, if necessary."

"It isn't necessary," Lee said, and took out his purse to pay. "But I thank you for the thought."

"Sorry if I spoke out of turn there," Mister Gruen said, "but you young men get into the damndest fixes sometimes. I hate to see it. This sort of country can be rough enough without a fine-looking young fellow going to seek out trouble he needn't."

"You have a point, certainly," Lee said, and had turned to the stairs to get his war-bag, Stetson, and rifle from his room, when someone came scratching at Gruen's back door.

Lee was starting up the stairs, when Gruen called to him.

"You have a visitor, Mister Lee!" He sounded amused.

When Lee came back downstairs, he saw an ugly Indian boy standing in Mister Gruen's kitchen—then saw that it was old Pebble's grandaughter, dressed in white man's trousers belted with a length of cord, a cheap flour sack shirt, knee-length moccasins, and a double thickness blanket coat that had been dark green when new.

The girl's brown face, narrow and big-nosed, was blank as the side of a wall—but perhaps from the way she stood, Lee knew the old man had died. She stood very lonely.

"He's dead?"

An abrupt head-shake. "Yes."

The girl said nothing more but stood looking up at Lee, as if waiting for something.

"I'll just leave you two alone," Mister Gruen said, and left his kitchen smiling and saying "Good lord," under his breath.

Lee realized Gruen thought the girl was some whore he'd met at Barkley's, come all the way to white-town to call. The girl had paid no mind to Gruen, only stood in the kitchen looking up at Lee, and seeming solitary as a prairie tree. Lee hoped this was no invitation to an Indian funeral. He'd been fond of the old man and had respected him, but he had neither the time nor the inclination to spend two or three days listening to Cree songs and eating dog stew.

Lee came down the stairs, took the girl by an arm wiry as telegraph line even through the thickness of her coat, and guided her out the kitchen door onto the back porch. There, she didn't try to pull away from him, but stood docile as a well-broken horse, looking at him sideways.

"Did the old man die well?" Lee said. "Did it hurt him badly to die?"

"It did not," the girl said, in her incongruous English. Seemed somewhat like a fox suddenly speaking. "He sing; he sleep; he die."

It sounded well enough. The old brave would enjoy no more amusements trailing with white men. Would have to obey no more last wishes of white men. Take no more journeys, too long, too difficult to survive, for white men.

Well enough.

"What do you do now?" Lee asked her. She seemed dressed to travel, and Pebble's paint stood rein-tied to Gruen's back porch.

"You have no guide," the girl said. She had white, slightly pointed teeth. Her breath frosted as she spoke, clouding for an instant before her face. It was a cold morning; the smell of snow weighed on the air. "You have no guide, now—but you have a guide again."

"You, I suppose," Lee said, and she shook her head briskly, "Yes."

Lee started to shake his head, too, then remembered, and nodded a "No." "The hell you are," he said, and meant it. "You need a stake, I'll give you one—within reason." (He wasn't sure she understand the "within reason" part of that, and amended it.) "I'll give you some money but not much."

The big-nose girl stared at him with that by now familiar alert dog look; then she said, "I want a ten dollars for guiding you into mountain. I want a ten dollars for guiding you out. I know where is the river where Big White Chief Surrey camps." Then she shut her mouth and watched Lee closely to see what he would say to that.

Lee said nothing for a moment, but reflected that in a fever or not, old Pebble had chattered what he shouldn't and been heard. Possible this girl saw only a chance to make some money guiding—some Indian women had done that job before. Possible also that if he refused her, she would go to that river where the White Chief camped and tell Surrey that Lee was coming.

"Do you know that country?" Lee said.

She held out two skinny brown fingers. "I go twice, with Papa." Meaning God knew who, her father or grandfather, Lee supposed. Truth was, he could certainly do better, *would* do better, to hire some Indian who really knew the country, had trapped it and hunted over it, and preferably a man who might back him in a fight, at least might if his own butt was in the pickling, too.

This girl filled no bill that way.

But she knew about Surrey. She knew about Lee. And what she knew, she might well go and tell.

"You're hired," Lee said. "Go to the stable, get my grey, and tack him out. We're leaving now." Then he went back into Albert's to get his possibles and ask Mister Gruen if he could board the wind-broke pack horse. Creature'd be of no use at a long fast run, and Lee had the notion he was due for some very swift running, him and a female guide, alone in quite unfriendly mountains.

Mister Gruen proving agreeable for a very small sum, Lee said his farewell, went out to the stable with his war-bag and rifle, and plundered the pack for anything handy and light to carry—the fry-pan, sack of coffee, sack of salt, sack of sugar, side of bacon, sack of corn meal. Had no good shirts, no clean trousers, no clean socks, no underwear.

Have to buy all that.

Lee looked at the girl, bending over the pack canvas by the last stall in a row, restowing Lee's goods fairly neatly. That stuff would be safe enough with Gruen . . .

nothing much to it for a happenstance thief.

A few minutes later, Lee and the girl rode out of Gruen's stable yard in fairly fine fettle —the grey prancing from his rest and three feeds of timothy and grain—cost to be added to the packy's board, and paid upon return. "Though I doubt Constable Ferguson will allow a prisoner's debts," Gruen had said, arranging his parlor antimacassars when Lee went in to say good-bye. Mister Gruen obviously thought Lee a fool not to be hopping to the border, and added, "I suspect your young 'friend,' beside being a terribly *ugly* savage, has fleas."

Lee laughed, shook Mister Gruen's hand, promised to return nevertheless, and asked him to look out for someone foolish enough to buy the pack-horse.

Lee and the girl rode out into a cold morning. By the time she'd led him to the town's prime dry goods, haberdashery, and sundry shop, it had begun to snow. Little swirling clouds of it blew past them as they rode. Lee stuck out his tongue and felt the faintest bite of tiny flakes. He glanced to the right and saw the Indian girl (What in God's name was her name? Patience? Hope? Some damn thing like that . . .) saw her watching him riding along with his tongue sticking out like a little boy with an all-day sucker in his mitt. In defiance, Lee kept his tongue out for a while longer. It was going to be tedious, traveling for days with a girl who stared at you as if she'd never seen the like before.

Lee suspected he was affording this skinny little squaw considerable amusement.

Patience? Not Patience . . . .

The dry goods was prime.

A big store, one of the biggest Lee had seen outside a good-sized town. Must be, he supposed, to service all the woods runners up here. Likely they came in once a year, traded their furs, and then bought the place out. Traps, whiskey, fire arms . . .

The proprietor, a burly French Jew named DuPont, was shifting stock when Lee and the girl came in, set down a keg of nails that must have weighed considerable, and came over to shake hands with Lee, introduce himself, and nod to the Indian girl. "Good morning, Miss Charity," he said to her, as nicely as if she was white, thus supplying Lee her name.

Lee caught the notion that DuPont knew of the trouble the night before at Barney Barkley's, but the store keeper said nothing of it, only ask what it was Lee needed.

"A whole damn fit-out of clothes," Lee said, already regretting he'd only brought two hundred dollars up in gold, and wondering if DuPont might be able to cash a draft on the Republican Bank of Boise, if it came to that. Lee'd seen the prices charged for soft goods in boom towns, and though *Eustache* didn't appear to be that flush, he was ready to be shocked by twenty-dollar pants and ten-dollar coffee pots, if those were the prices going.

But, no such.

DuPont's charges were much the same they would have been in Parker for the same goods—lower, some of them.

The store was divided into long, back-stretch halves shadowy as any cave toward the back, and two stories high, the goods packed and stacked and hung and piled in good order right along and up and down. Appeared to Lee a fellow if he had the cash could walk into DuPont's and walk out with anything at all he might require. There were barrels of long-handled tools at the front, and, by the cash-box, a case of firearms twenty feet long.

Place smelled of grease and gun oil, dyed cottons, cut wool, fur, sawn wood, and ready-mixed paints and wash. Fellow had himself a topper of a store—and, Lee noticed as DuPont led them down the aisle where the clothing (ready made) was hangered, folded, and stacked, that the store-keep carried a revolver tucked into his back trouser pocket, the better, no doubt, to discourage any drunken trappers from getting gay with his merchandise.

"I'll need two good wool shirts . . . set of underthings . . . two pairs of wool trousers. Some socks. A wool scarf—lamb's wool, if you have it. Sharpening stone . . . small hand ax . . . (Going into deep woods, would need that, sure.)

DuPont listened to Lee, took a single sharp look at him for sizes, then went straight to the proper stack, picked up the clothng, and laid it out for Lee to choose his colors. Lee chose dark, every time. No bright reds and yellows in the shirts, no white or stripes in the lamb's wool scarf.

Nothing to show up sharply in dark forest.

"You want those trousers tuck-sewed here and there?"

"No, thanks," Lee said. "I'm handy enough with a needle, if need be."

The shirts and trousers, the scarf, and a heavy pair of knit wool gloves to wear under his leather ones. Two pairs of washed-wool long johns. Three pairs of fine wool socks, double-knit. His boots would take a two-pair fit—be only a little tight, and the extra layer would keep him warmer. All these goods were of quality, and reasonable price.

The Indian girl stood by, watching Lee. She didn't finger any of the goods around her, didn't sort through anything, or window-shop them.

"I'll need a good match safe and the best sure-fire Lucifers you've got. A small coffee pot, a big fry pan, a tin kettle—very small, if you have one of those. Tin cup . . . two tin cups. Need one hundred rounds of forty-four-forty, little can of gun oil . . .''

"Graphite'd be better in this weather," DuPont said, and Lee agreed to take the powdered graphite rather than the oil.

"Neat's foot oil—little can. Two candles. Bar of soap . . . (Though heaven knew where he'd find water warm enough to wash in.) "And do you have ammunition for a fifty-caliber Sharp's?"

"I do," DuPont said, "and fine quality, too, though not much call for it."

"I'll take a box of forty, for extras," Lee said, and DuPont went behind the long gun case, pulled open a drawer back there, and was right out with just the ticket—Volcanic's Best Rifle Cartridge and Shot, Combined.

No saying there was not a pleasure, spending money. There was.

"I suppose I'll have new bandanna, too," Lee said. "Brown, if you stock that color—blue, if you don't." And some trail sweets . . . "Take a little sack of bull's eyes. Little sack of jaw-breakers. And I'll have two cans of peaches, two cans of tomatoes, and two cans of sardine fish."

"That be it?" DuPont said, still gathering the canned goods.

"No. I'll need a fur parka."

DuPont had the canned goods already out and stacked on his counter, was scooping the candies. "Wolf? Beaver? Mink?"

"What's warmest?"

"Wolf."

"Wolf it is—best you've got, please." No use freezing to death to save Surrey the necessity of killing him.

DuPont finished sacking the candy, took another hard look at Lee for size, and went off into the back for a minute or two. He returned carrying the handsomest parka Lee had ever seen—a soft heap of silver wolf fur, bone-toggled and hooded, lay over his arm.

"It's dear," DuPont said. "Thirty dollars. I have cheaper, and nearly as good."

"Hell, I'll take it," said the sport and big spender from the States. Occurred to Lee that he might be making a show of himself with this fancy a coat . . .

And that was that, for the buying.

Seventy-two dollars and change. A lot of horse-sale money to be going at once.

Lee sent the girl out for his saddle-bags, and DuPont was able to pack most of the stuff away, but had to provide an extra possibles sack for the canned goods and ammunition.

Lee shook the store keeper's hand— DuPont had a blacksmith's grip on him— then took the goods on out, the parka over his arm, the long silver fur stirring, shifting slightly in the faint breeze of his walking. A hell of a coat, and no mistake!

It was snowing harder when they got outside, and Lee made certain the girl tied the goods on tight behind the saddle-cantles. Didn't buy it, to lose it trailing.

135

He slipped the grey's reins from the hitch-post and swung on up—looked back to see the girl lashing the fry pan and coffee pot to the side of her saddle. Her bare hands looked thinner and darker than ever as she looped the rawhide and knotted it through a slow white swirl of falling snow. Coming down heavier and bigger flakes. Cold enough so that the flakes lay unmelted on the thin, worn wool of her coat.

Lee waited 'till she was done, and mounted on the paint, then led out down the rutted street at a jog trot. No use actually *waiting* for their damn constable.

He rode along two blocks and more, the girl (Charity) jogging along behind. Then he pulled the grey up and sat the saddle, considering. The snow was coming down like sixty now. Not much traffic on Main Street. A couple of lumber drays . . .

Sat the saddle a few moments more, the girl pulled up behind, waiting—then said "Shit!" Turned the grey's head, and rode right back the way he'd come.

Mister DuPont didn't look surprised to see him.

They rode out half an hour later. The Indian girl was fitted out with wool skirt, wool trousers (to be shortened on the trail) two wool shirts, cotton underthings ("They don't itch the ladies near as much," DuPont had said), wool socks, lamb's wool scarf, mittens, new moccasins, her own bar of soap, a tortoise shell comb, a fine hunting knife with a seven-inch blade, and—Lee figured he'd better arm her, or blame himself later for not—a brand new Winchester lever-action rifle. A thirty caliber. Too light a piece for Lee's liking, but about right for a girl Indian weighed about a hundred pounds.

All that cost him a sight of money, and Lee was relieved that DuPont had no wolf parkas small enough to fit her. Had to make do with beaver, wool-lined.

By God, I hope you're satisfied! Lee said to himself as they rode up-slope and out of town, the grey farting his morning farts. *I hope you're satisfied, spending that sort of money, and for what? So a goddamn Cree Indian will think you're a jackass—that's for what!*

Now was that all. A fat and sleepy whore had been roused out into the alley behind Barney Barkley's (Charity had gone in to wake her and call her out) to receive a rock crystal necklace as a gift, a rock crystal necklace that had cost Lee nine dollars and fifty cents at DuPont's.

Riding out of that alley leaving a fat, red-skinned, sateen-wrapped whore weeping, clutching her bauble, Lee determined that he was single-handed keeping the store keeper in business, and commencing the enrichment of the Cree nation as well.

By midafternoon the snow had stopped, and Lee followed Charity's lead along the timber line of a mountain twice the size of the Old Man at home. It was high country, and cold, and they rode into a wind that stung at Lee's face huddled into his fine new scarf like a swarm of bees.

To their left, the land fell away in great steep swoops, stairways for a race of giants who might, in hundred-yard strides, go thundering down that deep. To Lee's right, the cliffs rose up granite grey and sheer as hanging curtains, higher than a rifle shot, to still more cliffs above, lifting into the sky's haze, as cold and granite colored as the stone. These huge faces had fractured here and there and spired into pinnacles and towers, then sunk at some distant heights into deep and sudden caverns, gaping like the roosts of owls big as houses high on wide rock walls.

The wind came buffeting and gave no rest; twice, both the grey and paint had tried to stop and turn their butts to it for poor shelter.

Lee, feeling that if this was the start of winter in this country, then the rest of that season would be something to behold, had second and third thoughts about the big-nosed girl as guide. She had insisted on riding high, rather than following the river road through the forests.

"Too many," she'd said, when Lee had asked her why. "Too many." Meaning, he had supposed, that too many travelers took that road. Too many travelers who might notice and talk about a Yankee out riding after Lord Surrey's camp. Perhaps, also, too many woods-runners who might back-shoot and murder venturers with good horses under them and warm clothes on their backs.

She might have meant that. Or she might have meant evil spirits—way too many of those—or ghosts of ancestors, or unappeased animal souls, hunted and not apologized to. There was no way of telling what went on behind those anthracite eyes, that beak of a nose, that narrow brow. Homely as a hedge fence and, more than likely, no proper guide at all.

Lee booted the grey a tad to the right—the fool beast was curious, it seemed, and leaned between wind gusts to look down into the pitchy valley below. A hard trail, but the girl had seemed to know it and did not appear to be frightened by it. She rode ahead, back straight as a cavalryman's—fine saddle-sitting for a woods Indian—and seemed un-worried by the uncertainty of the trail, or by the weather either. Not, of course, that she had need to be, considering the fine woolens and furs she was wearing. Truth was, far as clothing went, they were both snug as bugs in rugs.

It was the possibility of a fall and a busted horse leg that worried Lee. That happen, they would be in sore straits . . .

The girl had paused on the first steep rise hours before, pulled the stocky paint to a halt, and pointed back and down.

Lee, turning in his sasddle, had seen far, far below them the short, thin, little black worm of *Eustache*, where the town straggled for its quarter mile along the merest slight section of the mountain's skirt.

A far piece.

Ahead, the girl and paint horse turned a rock-shelf corner to the right and disappeared. Lee touched the grey with his left-side spur to quicken him and keep him to the right. Occurred to him that Surrey might already know of some such likelihood as Dowd's friend coming north. It was possible that Dowd's dying babble had been heard and noted. Possible, too, that Surrey or his cannibal Frenchman had caught old Pebble in his brush hidey and squeezed out of him the tale they'd let him carry south.

Lee had no notion of believing he knew all that had happened at Dowd's camp. No notion, either, that this big-nosed girl was as simple as she seemed.

It was a question of choice, that was all.

He had chosen, first, to come up—on the fact of Dowd's death, most of all.

Surrey was a cause in that for sure. The cannibal Frenchman, too. And if old Pebble or this stick of a girl happened to be a bait—

so be it. Time would tell whether the trap would hold the bear.

CHAPTER SIX

That night and the night thereafter they camped high. The first night, the girl found a fallen pine weathered more than half to punk, and wedged down in a rock crack ten feet deep.

The new winter wind poured over that ditch like a river, and if either Lee or the girl stood up, they were buffeted, the girl sent staggering. But the punk wood burned to a fine red-crusted roar, heating the cleft to hot at least where it was deepest.

Difficult to think of a finer trail camp in such weather. Would have been no good at all in rain, no good in hard heat—but for a bitter, raw wind, salted with snow, none better.

The girl had set to shifting for supper right away—had sliced the bacon and after that, discovered in the possibles sack a gift of a dozen of last morning's biscuits from Mister Gruen tucked in, likely, while Lee spoke to the Indian girl on Gruen's back porch. Lee's lie about not preferring beaten biscuits had produced its reward. The bacon sliced, the biscuits tucked down near the coals to warm, the girl had shaken canteen water—no need to conserve what the sky was flurrying down —over a tin plate of corn meal, and commenced to mix corn cakes into a frying batter. Then, the bacon into the pan, sizzling until half-cooked and shoved aside for the corn cakes to fry in the fat. Poked and prodded, then tested and tasted from the gleaming point and edge of her new knife.

When it was done—bacon crisp, with an edge of popping fat to line each slice, corn cakes puffed and browning, smelling like summer—the girl parceled it out on tin pie plates (salvaged by her from the horse-pack), and set the coffee in the fire to rumble to a ready boil and be yanked as swiftly out. She pulled a can of peaches from Lee's saddlebags, hacked off the top of it, and set it out to be drunk and eaten from.

After that dinner, Lee no longer regretted the spree at DuPont's store, or resented the clothes and parka he had felt he must buy the girl. The Big-nose girl threw a better camp than Pebble had, and Pebble had been no slouch at trailing.

The heat of the burning fallen log was such

that neither had to wrap in a buffalo robe, but only stretch out on it, like a gentleman and lady in back garden hammocks. Through the night, just above their heads, the bitter wind went blowing, but not upon them.

One of the best camps Lee had known.

The second high camp was a different kettle of fish.

It came, for one thing, after a longer day's riding and a day's riding higher than the day before, so that the horses panted as they climbed, and Lee found his mouth and throat so dry that he had to drink water time and again to ease that dryness. The girl drank a good deal of water, too, and Lee heard her cough a time or two when she rode short in the lead.

Still, she seemed to know her way and, unlike her grandfather, appeared to take no delight in finding rough ways out to test Lee's riding, or his fine grey's carrying. She guided for the smoothest way, and precious little there was of smoothness on that no-name mountain's shoulder.

By the second evening, Lee and the girl were both dismounted, leading their horses skidding and clattering along a ledge barely wide enough. The light was leaving them— the last of the day barely bright enough to reveal the miles on miles of dark green forest stretching out from the western slopes of the mountains. There was, or seemed to be, a break in that expanse, the fading mirror-gleam of a lake two, three days ride away—and that only after the edge forest was reached.

There were darker lines coiling through the distant woods. Rivers, apparently, but not wide enough to show as more than dark partings in the wilderness of trees.

Earlier, Charity had pointed out one of those leagues-away oxbows, said, *"Sansakootch,"* or something like it for the river's name, and added that White Chief Surrey was encamped there, measuring out the land. Surveying, Lee assumed.

It looked to be a hell of a far piece.

The ledge they were leading along now looked to be too long a piece itself. Lee wondered if Big-nose had lost her way and was scared to admit it. Soon enough, it would be too dark to try and turn the horses, get back to wider ground. The wind was down, which was a mercy, but if anything it was even colder than it had been the day before . . . cold that worked and pried at a man, to weary him and bite into his bones.

Lee heard a dim thundering—seemed to rise and fall to some sort of rhythm—not like weather thunder at all. He looked sharp and looked up, thinking that an avalanche might be coming down on them. But the cliffs above were clear, as well as he could see in the failing light. If the light dimmed much more, he was liable—and the girl that much more liable—to lead his horse straight over the shelf's edge into empty air.

That thundering . . . it stirred the mass of rock under his feet, vibrated and shook it. Perhaps an avalanche ahead—and if so, the squaw appeared willing to lead on into it.

"Say! SAY—GOD-DAMNIT!" He saw her stop walking, turn, and look back at him past the paint's shoulder. Could barely make that out, it was getting so dark.

Lee dropped the grey's reins rather than crowd him forward into the paint's butt, trusting the horse to stay ground-tied for a minute without going to try and fly off the ledge, and edged his way up alongside the paint to the Cree girl.

"What in hell's that noise?" He cupped his hand to his ear to demonstrate "noise."

The skinny thing gave him that look of hers, a stare made odder from under the hood of the beaver parka, shrugged, and said, "Water . . . falling." She made a graceful falling gesture with her free hand, the other fast to the paint's rein.

"Waterfall."

She shook her head. "Yes."

Lee shook his head, too, but meant no "Yes" by it. He walked carefully back to the grey, which had had the smarts to stay put, and gathered up its reins.

When he looked back, the girl was still watching him, apparently for instructions, and Lee waved her on. It was too late and too dark now to be turning back. Night might catch them on the ledge ahead or under that falls but it would certain sure catch them on the ledge if they turned back now.

One thing, though—the girl knew the trail, had been on it before. "Falling water . . ." And a graceful wrist to go with it. Damn shame about that nose. Gave her a proud look, though, if a man could get used to the *size* of the thing.

Lee saw her up ahead tugging at the paint's leather to get him moving, then turning to lead the animal on. Lee hauled the reluctant grey on after. The big horse was pleased enough to be ridden. Didn't care to be led. As they moved, creeping along the rock shelf as cautious as maiden aunts, the horses snorting and trembling, clattering uneasily along, Lee heard the thundering of the falls grow louder. The stone vibrated under his boot soles as it were being struck with great hammers. Thing must run close . . .

Ahead, Charity led the pinto up a shallow fall, then on. Lee saw the pinto's tail switching, the white splotches on its butt just visible. Going to be time to camp up, and soon. Time you can't see a half-white horse not twenty feet from you is the time to get off a mountain sheer and camp up. Trouble was, Lee saw no sign of the ledge widening, not in an hour and more of leading along it.

No sign of the pinto at all now, and Lee

stepped out a little, but carefully, keeping his eye to the left, following the line of the shelf edge there. Not in that much of a hurry that he wanted to sail on down two thousand feet and more to light hard at the tree-line.

No sign of the pinto—and he stepped a little faster, guiding, before he realized it, by the gleam of wet on the granite ledge.

Led around a ragged corner of stone, a corner a foot to his right that rose straight up and out of sight in darkness. It was night now and no mistake.

As he cleared that corner, the grey shaking his head, holding back, Lee was struck by a cloud of ice water spray that soaked him ass to tea kettle in a flash.

With it, a crash of sound.

Already wet, and too late to worry about that, Lee saw the pinto's light colored hide huddled against the mountain wall a yard or two ahead, and past the horse (and Indian girl holding its halter) saw a blacker blackness than the night had to offer, arching up and out over their heads—and farther, twenty feet out from the ledge. A black river, gleaming as poured oil, launched itself from high above, and poured in that terrific torrent over them . . . and far out . . . and down and down and down through the air. It thundered and struck the mountain's stone as it leaped . . . and was so black. Not any trace of foam marred its blackness once it was launched out, arching over them. A black, rushing river, falling away into black night air. It was impossible to see or hear where it fell down there, or if it fell and struck at all short of those empty thousands of feet.

It was the damndest thing . . .

And they were soaked through—furs, clothes, sacks and saddle-bags. The horses were soaked.

And this on a mountain height, and that colder than the Seventh Circle. The Redskin bitch had blundered enough to freeze them dead. His fault, though. He'd let her lead too long, tired, and she'd remembered the falls being still another turn ahead, been surprised and soaked in iced water before she knew it.

Wouldn't matter who was at fault, though. Get out of this quick or die for the error.

Lee hauled the grey up closer, reached out to seize the girl's sopping furs and dragged her to him to shout in her ear over the smashing of the falls above.

"WHAT'S AHEAD? WHAT'S PAST THIS FALL?"

The girl—he could barely make out her face—shouted back, "SAME!" meaning, Lee devoutly hoped, more ledge, and not more falling water. He felt her trembling under his hand—freezing and tired, and out of grit—and so would he be if he stood drenched under that river for long.

Lee gave the Cree a savage shake to stir her. "COME ON AFTER ME!" Without waiting to see if she understood or would follow, he yanked the grey's rein and towed the tall horse along after him beneath that over-arching flood, slipping and stumbling through icy showers over heaps of rubble on that dark and narrow way. He kept his right shoulder to the rock wall, hauled the grey's head down when the animal whinnied and made to rear in the darkness, and threatened to shoot the beast there and then—a promise unheard in the appalling freight train noise of the river that ran overhead.

It seemed a long run in the dark.

Lee tripped over a low rock-shelf, fell to his knees, and staggered to his feet fast, not wanting the grey to lunge over him, kick him. A few more steps, the horse coming along pretty well, scared quiet by the dark and noise, and Lee climbed up another shallow shelf, the grey coming up right behind him—and found himself out of the freezing spray. The crashing noise was muffled to a grinding roar. Turned some sort of a corner there and he was thankful for it.

He held the grey close and turned to try and see the girl. Would have been easy enough for her to walk straight over that edge or be yanked over by the paint in panic.

Nothing. Nothing coming along the narrow ledge out of the dark.

He'd have to leave the grey. Leave him standing, and go back for that damn squaw.

Lee dropped the horse's reins, put his left hand out to find the side of the mountain, and started walking back along the ledge, back into the thunder of the torrent. He could see nothing . . . feel the wet stone wall under his left hand, the rough stones and rubble under his boots. *Keep left, or fall.*

The girl walked into him out of the dark. Didn't know she was there 'till she smacked into him, soaked fur, skinny arms, big nose and all. The paint loomed shadowy-light behind.

The grey was waiting where he'd been left, too frightened to move off in the dark, likely. Lee picked up his reins, and led out. It was get clear of that icy water misting down, spraying the ledge from side to side from the falls, or freeze in the night and die.

Not more than a hundred feet further down the ledge, Lee found the shelf just slightly wider, near as he could tell probing out to the edge with the Sharp's long barrel. Dark as the inside of a sack. Back of this stretch, in the mountain wall, was a long, shallow niche, not more than a foot or two high, the same in depth.

It wasn't much. Maybe not enough, if the night got even colder. Ice rimmed the fur of Lee's parka; he had felt it with his fingers, crusted down the mountain's stone. *Maybe not enough* . . . But no choice at all about it. Try leading on out across this ledge in pitch dark, and freezing—they'd go over. They'd fall or die of the cold.

No choice left on that. Camp in here or say good-bye.

It was no slice of pie, even so. The only dry things they had were the buffalo robes still rolled under the slickers behind their saddles. Lee reached out for the girl in the dark—she was stumbling on the ledge as if she were drunk—got a hold of her, and shouted into her ear what he wanted her to do. The sounds of the river were lower now, but still rumbled through the air like drums.

Together in the dark, keeping as near the mountain wall as they could, Lee and the girl hauled the two horses in close to that long niche in the stone, found Lee's lariat-coil at his saddle-bow, slipped the line through both animals' halters, and knotted it short to hold them close together. Then Lee hobbled them, stripped the saddles, cut the frozen rawhide lashings on the slicker rolls, and tugged out the buffalo robes to spread out along the niche's shallow length. Lee's hands lost all feeling as he worked; he had to put his face down to them once in the dark to feel where he held his knife . . . where the blade was. The steel burned his face like fire.

When he'd finished, Lee had to search for the girl again, stumbling over the stones, yelling for her. He thought she might have gone over the edge, and was crouching, feeling his way to out across the ledge, when he found her lying curled on her side, shaking. He stood, pulled her to her feet, slapped her across the face, and shoved her back toward the mountain wall. He followed her there, took hold of her, dragged her stumbling in behind the hobbled horses, and stripped the ice-stiff clothing off her. He stripped her naked—she was narrow-built as a child—then pushed her down into the stone niche, into the folds of the buffalo robes. Her skin had seemed cold as the stone itself to him.

Then he pulled his own clothes off. Wet to the skin and trembling, barely able to bend his fingers. It took a time to do. The furs, the wool shirt and trousers, his underwear, socks and boots were all frozen stiff as cardboard and crackled with ice as he dragged them off.

If there were any wind at all up here, he and the girl would be dead as doornails already. No wind (and that unusual, so high) and the robes kept dry in their slicker rolls. . . These gave them their only chance.

Lee managed to get most of the girl's clothes together with his own, and spread the parkas and other pieces he could find across the horses' backs as they shifted together in the dark, snorting. He got the stuff on them, and he found the possibles sack, got out lashing line, and corded the clothes across the horses' backs.

He did it stark naked, and freezing, and in the dark—and it was the hardest thing to do that he had ever done. The only chance, though, to get those goods dry by morning. And those goods had better be dry by morning, or dry enough to wear, or God Almighty help them!

CHAPTER SEVEN

The next day, they led the horses over the mountain's hump and on down to the tree-line—still very high, but not as high as before.

They were both tired as trolley-horses. Lee's bones felt like hollow sticks, stumping along. Only good thing was, the grey was weary too, too tired to act up. The country around them was slowly leveling out, thank God. Lee had always loved the mountains and had ridden high in them many times, but never had gotten into such a fix as last night's.

That one had damn near killed him. Still felt cold and every stitch he had on felt nearly damp as a dish-rag but just dry enough to wear.

The girl had perked up fine, though, as far

as you could tell with Indians. Had spent the night wrapped around him, buck naked and skinny as a San Francisco organ grinder's monkey. Cold as a dish of iced-cream, too. Creature didn't ever seem to warm up. Then, bright and early in the dawn, damned if she didn't wake up and get up, bright as a new penny (about the same color, too) and set to doing the horses, and then a foul cold breakfast that Lee was grateful to eat.

That ledge, in daylight, was enough to frighten a general—not more than five or six feet wide and paved with sharp stone trash, and this their refuge and safety in the night.

The big-nose girl—*what the hell was her name?* Charity. Charity'd picked right up, hadn't made any excuse for guiding them into that tight, for not stopping well short of the falls—had just picked right up and gone to guiding. Taken them over the rest of the mountain.

Lee'd stepped to the lead then—any fool could see the way past timberline. He was pleased the manner the grey and paint had come through that cold night and done some clothes drying while they were at it. Poor as that packy had been—a sad representative of Spade Bit stock—poor as he'd been, the grey and paint were fine and better than fine. Couldn't ask for sweeter stayers than these horses.

The distant river that marked the forest in its dark, winding line, was closer now.

Looked to be no more than two, three day's ride away. Then . . . then it would be time to skin the cat. Lee had been wondering how it was that little Dowd got caught so short . . . had not gone better guarded to do his land-buying business against the interests of the young English Lord, it seemed. Been thinking about that, climbing down the steeps—seeing some shrub and mosses, now, the dwarf pines beginning a few hundred feet further down. (Nice hot day—damn cold, was the truth—but *seemed* hot as biscuits after a night on that ledge!)

Lee'd been thinking about it—why the little man had been so incautious—and now thought he knew. Old Gruen had given him the hint, with all that about history. Dowd had been Canadian, had been raised to respect those ancient English families. Lord Surrey. Son of a Duke! A real English Earl.

What fellow raised more British-than-not would think that an Earl would as quick to kill for his profit as any back-alley bully for a five-dollar piece?

Little Dowd should have remembered his history better and recalled just how those fine families had gotten their lands and noble titles. With what play of swords and axes. What knives in the dark . . .

So there'd be no long parley at Surrey's camp. The boy would likely be as quick to take Lee's measure as Dowd's and come to the same conclusion of killing—or trying to.

No delay with that cannibal trapper, either. The English boy would keep that creature close to guard him, might suspect—if he didn't know—that some friend of Dowd's might come calling. Charity had called the trapper a *loup-garou*, some sort of werewolf, she thought, near as Lee could make out. Scared her, that was for sure. Lee'd heard it took silver bullets to kill those creatures. In this case, steel or lead would have to do.

Surprise wouldn't be in it, that was for sure. Lee had no notion of coming close through a trapper's forest without the trapper knowing.

They'd know he was coming, the last day or so.

As well, though, they didn't know earlier—know soon enough to set a dead-fall of some kind for him. Meant no hunting, no gunshots to echo from the mountains. Could snare some early snowshoes, likely, roast them on sticks with some bacon stuffed into them. That would be about it for the hunting, next two or three days.

Not a bad day for weather, either. Cold but clear enough for good seeing, and still none of that hard, steady wind that had shoved at them first night out. A few clouds like sailing ships, way off to the west. Silver-white. No look of rain to them.

No. Not much use of playing French detective—the Lupin fellow. No use playing him or a Pinkerton with this fine young Lord and his

cannibal friend. Sure to be quick doings . . .
Lee felt satisfied enough with that. Wasn't
frightened by the notion, in any case. Likely
had all the scare scared out of him by that
brute in Barney Barkley's. If that underhand
throw had missed, the man might well have
carved Lee to a Sunday roast. Big enough.
Tough enough, too.

Not a bad day, if he'd had more sleep and
less shivering. Woke with a hard-on, too,
right smack up against the Indian girl's
skinny belly. She hadn't appeared to take
notice of it, and he'd turned away from her.
Whoever said a boner had no conscience?
One of the Latin authors, Lee thought. Professor Riles had quoted the man to him once,
in his cups. Damned if he could remember
which one . . . Catullus, maybe, though that
seemed too pat.

Some advantage, Lee supposed, to even an
incompleted education.

He was walking, leading down among
thick-grown scrub pine now. The true
timberline beginning. It felt good to be away
from only rock and stones, to be back among
green growing things again, even these short,
dense, paltry trees. Lee heard a marmot
whistle in some alarm up ahead. Likely the
shadow of a hawk had frightened it. Be time
soon for the marmots to start sleeping in for
the winter.

Lee stopped walking, held the grey's halter
for a moment to steady him, then set his

boot toe in the stirrup and swung up. "Time for you to do some of the work . . ." Safe enough riding from here—the track was gentle, at least what could be seen of it through the small crowded pines.

Lee looked back and saw the girl leading down; the paint was behaving well. No reason she shouldn't mount up, too. The lord only knew they'd walked their share.

Lee dug into his war-bag for the coils of his whip, pulled the black-snake out, shook out the fine, black braided leather, and commenced, with easy swings of his arm, to shake out the lash, and then, for practice and while thinking, to pop the leather at the stands of little trees he passed snipping morsels off here and there.

He had not thought of S'ien for a day and more.

He had just realized that, and was wondering what it meant when the grey screamed, reared straight up, whirled, and threw Lee ass over tea-cup into the greenery.

The pines were growing thick at this height, and they were there in plenty but there was no brushy ground beneath them. Lee hit stony soil, and he hit it hard. Heard the grey galloping as he lay there, heard the Indian girl—Charity—heard Charity shouting. Lee thought if his neck was broken, he'd know it, so thought it wasn't. He was lying on his face—felt marked up there more than a little—and said "God damnit!" turned over, and got up onto his knees. Still had the whip clutched in his hand. Damn nothing else. His hat had flown off. Revolver gone. Lee didn't try to stand up for a moment, afraid he'd find he'd broken a leg, at least, if not his neck. One of the worst falls he'd even taken off a horse—*That wood-headed grey son-of-a-bitch! Better be the biggest rattler in the world scared him or the biggest wasp bit him in the ass. Better be!*

Lee wiggled his feet in his boots; legs seemed all right. He was starting to feel a fool, on his knees here. The girl would think he was a damn fool.

Lee stood up but he took his time about it. A rattling fall, and no mistake.

He looked up-trail, and saw that Charity had managed to catch the grey when he ran by her—still having a hard time holding him, though; paint jumping around up there, too. Girl was staring at Lee with her mouth wide open. Looked like a baby bird, with that big beak. Guess she never saw a fellow flying before!

Lee heard a grunt, turned and saw a grizzly bear—a big bear the color of cinnamon. It was up on its hinds not forty feet away, its paws folded to its chest, and was looking at him, weaving its head slowly from side to side like a near-sighted man trying to make something out.

The girl shouted, and Lee knew what she would do next. He turned just as she was hauling her brand new Winchester repeater out of its scabbard at the paint's shoulder. Hard doings, too; both horses were dancing around her, trying to get her between them and the bear.

We'll get out of this, Lee thought, if that squaw doesn't start shooting. Might as well send Surrey a telegraph message as start firing rifle shots in these mountains!

He gestured "No"—couldn't remember to nod or shake his head, and finally shouted, "No shooting, God damnit!"

The bear didn't care for that shouting—likely had been out on the mountain hunting marmots for his winter sleep. Didn't like the shouting at all.

Lee heard the bear squeal—exactly the sound a huge pig might have made—turned, and saw the animal drop suddenly to all fours, almost out of sight in the dwarf pines, and come for him.

Lee was astonished how fast that huge beast moved. It came galloping, crashing through the little pines as if they'd been prairie grass. It looked like a great gold-brown rug, suddenly animated and made furious and given the power to charge, fronted with a gaping, wrinkled black muzzle packed with yellow teeth.

The bear champed its jaws, squealed like the father of all pigs and came for him.

Lee spun and ran to the right, conscious as he did it that he was running faster than he ever had—much faster than most men could run. Right after that, he wished the girl would disobey him, and shoot at the thing. . .

He heard the dense little pines smash right behind him, spun again with the whip still in his hand, and threw out a desperate coil to lash at the beast.

It was great good luck, and only luck, that he struck the creature's muzzle a sharp *crack* of the lash. The bear must have jerked its head aside at the sting of that, though so quickly that Lee didn't see it. Perhaps the sharp snapping sound so close to its ear threw it off its balance. But whichever, it shifted in its stride, struck Lee a glancing blow with a paw, too quick a movement for Lee to clearly see, and knocked him away ten feet, his left arm dead as mutton.

He thought he heard the girl scream.

Rooting sounds . . . snorting, rooting sounds. *Now . . . what in hell?* Lee woke up all the way as if from a terrible dream and heard the girl screaming in earnest and the sounds the bear made a few yards away. Damn animal!

Lee got to his feet and stood steady enough. He didn't feel so bad. Left arm was gone—Lee glanced down—was numb. Still had the whip.

The bear was making no noise. How could such a big animal get out of sight in the pine thickets? Lee took a slow, careful step back. Might be able to run. Might do that, and get clear . . . call to the girl from further down in the trees . . .

Lee took another slow, careful step back. Was sorry the moment he did it. It made a noise.

The bear stood up out of the pine scrub not much more than fifteen feet away and stared down at Lee. Its head was huge, looking two feet wide. The eyes were very small. They didn't look like a dog's eyes. They looked like a stupid person's eyes, set in an awful head.

Lee was so frightened he felt sick. The girl had stopped screaming.

Do something! Do something—or run like a rabbit, and listen to the bear catch up.

Lee drew back his right arm, yelled with the effort, and lashed at the bear with all his strength, the long coil of the whip leaping out, the tiny, lead-weighted tip striking the animal straight across the snout.

The beast snorted and shook its head and then took two rolling steps forward on its hind legs, its massive weight swaying from side to side. There was foam on the side of its muzzle.

Lee struck at it again. Long whip-lash whined through the air and caught the bear alongside its head, just below its ear.

The beast bawled at that, and shook its head again, suddenly snapping to the side, as if at an insect that had bitten it. But it watched Lee's right arm. Lee could smell the thing; it smelled of rotten meat.

Lee felt the bear would kill him, sure; and more in anger over this than out of courage, he drew back his arm and whipped at the animal again. But this time, in a wonderfully quick way, the bear, even awkward on its hind legs, swayed away from the flickering lash, and was not touched.

The whip, all Lee's strength behind it, cracked on empty air.

That sound appeared to frighten the animal as the slicing stroke of the lash had not. The grizzly looked down at Lee a moment more, its great head cocked to the side as if to inquire about that sharp and sudden sound.

Lee stood and looked back—hadn't the strength to do a damn thing more. Was run out of sand. Out of piss, too. Lee felt the wetness of his crotch.

The bear went to all fours more gracefully than any human could do anything and disappeared, sunk into the green thicket of stunted pines only fifteen feet away.

Lee thought he heard him . . . was certain he heard him coming. Coming slowly . . .

It seemed to take a very long time. Lee would have preferred the bear come standing, where he could see him. It was tiring, waiting to be killed, and not seeing anything.

Lee stood there, stood still, until the Indian girl called to him. He'd been staring into the thick growth of pines and was reluctant to raise his eyes from the green to look for her.

He didn't want the bear to surprise him. He wanted to see it coming.

The Indian girl called to him again.

Slowly . . . slowly, Lee looked up, and saw her perhaps a hundred yards away. She stood with the two horses. They still pranced around her, sidling and tugging at the reins. Nothing seemed to have changed over there at all. It was as if the bear had faced Lee only for an instant.

The girl pointed away, down the mountain. Pointed again, and made a swift, rippling, traveling sign with her fingers.

Lee heard himself breathing in and out . . . in and out. It appeared that the grizzly was gone.

The first thing he felt was a terrible anger at the girl for not shooting at it. That seemed for a few moments to be something unforgiveable. Lee felt like killing her for it. He remembered very well telling her not to fire and he remembered very well why that was important, but all that seemed beside the point.

The point was, she should have shot that bear—should certainly have shot *at* it.

He was too angry to talk to her for some time. He waded through the shoulder-high stand of pines to catch up the grey's reins from her, and, despite his left arm which felt asleep, numb and full of prickles, he managed to climb aboard the horse, and after a moment was able to spur it slightly and make it walk down toward the trail. He didn't care a damn if she'd seen he'd pissed his pants.

There, where the grey had reared, Lee rode in small circles, looking for his Stetson and the Bisley Colt's. He didn't trouble to take the Sharp's out of the rifle boot. He wasn't thinking of the bear, but only about the girl's stupidity in not shooting at it.

He found the revolver first—a piece of luck, because it had fallen under one of the pines, and was hard to see. The Stetson took longer and he was about to give up on it, when he saw a particular shade of grey within some green, and that turned out to be the hat. It had sailed a ways. Lee picked up both revolver and hat by leaning down from the saddle. He didn't feel like getting off the horse, and mounting up again. Seemed like too much work.

He put on his hat, set it firmly on his head, and turned the grey downhill again. To hell with the girl—she could follow on or not. Stupid savage, standing there with that Winchester in her hands. Damned if he knew what he had bought her the rifle for if she was too dumb to use it.

He found, as he rode, that he had a headache that got worse instead of better. Seemed to be cracking his head wide open . . . hurt so bad, it made him sick to his stomach.

More than a mile down the trail with the Indian girl riding well behind Lee felt too sick to stay on the horse. He pulled the grey up, climbed down, stood bent over, his hands braced on his knees, and vomited up his breakfast. He thought as he did it that maybe his heart was coming up as well, he felt that bad.

When he was finished, he stayed bent over a little longer, trying to get a true deep breath. His heart was running like a locomotive on a track. Damn hard to get a deep breath into him.

Stayed right there for a while. Seemed as though that bear had been a bad dream, fast as it had happened. Just a bad dream, and that was all . . .

The girl, Charity, rode up and sat her horse, watching him. Lee knew she was there but didn't care to look at her. Having her fun, he supposed, to see a white man had pissed his pants from fear and lost his breakfast from it, too.

"Bear-whipper," the girl said, from the paint's saddle. "No man has been so brave as that . . ."

Lee heard that stuff and didn't think much of it, but he stood up straight, at the least. Showed what a fool the girl was—how young she was—to be spouting horse-shit like that. He unknotted his bandanna and wiped his mouth with it. Wouldn't be much of a Roland with vomit on his chin.

"Don't be a damn fool," he said to the Indian girl. " That animal scared me half to death, and you know it." He went to the grey, shaking his left arm to get more life into it. It still stung and prickled, felt more than half asleep.

"Yes," the Indian girl said, "one side scared; other side, brave."

"Why don't you be quiet?" Lee said and using his right hand and arm, hauled himself up into the saddle. It occurred to him that if the bear had hit his right shoulder, he'd be out of the revolver-drawing business, maybe forever. As it was, a sad left arm would be of little help down in that forest, little help against Surrey and his French friend.

He spurred the grey on out through the dwarf pines, feeling a little better than he had. Better for the vomiting, likely.

CHAPTER EIGHT

That night at last they camped off the mountain.

They rode down off the stone in early evening, down through fields of autumn-browned brush, into the first big trees. The evening was cold, and now, as if it had waited until they were off the mountain, the wind sprang up and came whistling through the hemlocks and great pines to ruffle the horses' manes, tug at the brim of Lee's Stetson. A cold wind, with the colder smell of snow on it.

These trees, even at the mountain's foot, were big enough, tall enough, for each to have cleared around itself a space bare of other growth or brush, carpeted with soft needles deep enough to muffle the sounds of the horses' hooves. It made for quiet riding—

and all the better, Lee thought. The quieter, the better. He rubbed his left arm as they rode through dusky tree-shade. The cold wind made his left shoulder ache.

Riding into these trees was easy enough. Perhaps riding out would be more difficult.

Charity cooked bacon and sugar-flour for him for supper—refused that dainty sweet herself. Had candy, then, the two of them. Sitting in a forest as lost as Atlantis, he still stiff from a monster's paw, they gobbled bull's eyes and jaw breakers like kids.

The wind died again by full dark, and the still, silent cold came settling down through the trees.

Lee lay in his buffalo robe, trying to ease the ache in his left shoulder, in the muscle of his back. Felt as if he'd gone full rounds with the Champion. This forest air smelled better than good—the odor of pine as rich as toilet-water, but cleaner by the nostrils, somehow. Cleaner. Odd, how after such a fright by a great wild creature he felt no fear at all of this forest dark. It was as if a man had only so much fear in him and could exhaust it, run out of fear as men sometimes ran out of courage. If that was true, then sure as God made little green apples, he had scraped the bottom of his barrel of that commodity. The bear had taken all fear from him—at least for a while.

Lee lay thinking of other times, sunnier country. Other people, too. Some living.

Most of them, dead. Didn't make him sad,
though, thinking of the dead ones. His father
. . . and Harvey Logan. That small pimp, out
behind Blackie's in San Francisco. Catherine
Dowd . . . S'ien.

Didn't make him sad. It made him . . . consider matters. Appeared that being near eaten
by a bear made for philosophy. Life and the
puzzles of life. Jig-saw puzzles, was what
they were . . .

He was just slipping into sleep when the
Big-nosed girl came to him in the dark.

She woke him when she left her robe
across the fire's embers. He heard her getting
up, stepping softly over the pine needle
carpet. She came to him around the fire. He
turned his head and saw her in the embers'
glow, buck naked and skinny as a grass stalk
in the faint, warm light. Shame about her
nose . . . Slanted eyes, much like S'ien's,
really. No question at all those people were
relatives of some sort—the Indians and
Orientals. Too like not to be.

Little fur on her narrow cunt that he could
see—almost bare, and soft, the slit pouted
tight shut as any child's. Her tender breasts,
in ember-light, were delicate, barely budded,
but tipped with the fat, brown nipples of a
woman.

"Go on back over there," Lee said to her.
"Get in that robe there or you'll freeze your
butt."

She said nothing to that, but came to him,

bent down and drew back his cover and slid in beside him bare as a nut. Her skin was smooth as glass and icy cold from only that short walk.

"You're not much comfort," Lee said, "cold as that. I was more comfortable without you." She turned on her side to him under the buffalo robe and commenced to rub at his sore left arm and shoulder. Her hand was cold, too. "More comfortable by a damn sight." But she continued that rubbing, and it felt well enough, seemed to help the arm a bit, being rubbed like that. His shoulder ached more than a little, though. She was digging her fingers into the muscles there, felt like she was trying to dig the ache right out of him.

Felt all right. Felt pretty good, really . . . Hurt sometimes, when she gripped too hard but all in all, felt pretty good. He turned a little so that she could get at his shoulder-blade and she slid her fingers up his back there, drew the line of the blade-bone with her fingertips, then pressed harder, as if she could push the pain out of him, force the stiffness and soreness out.

"Not so hard."

She eased off then but only for a while, then began stroking harder, pressing harder. This time it felt all right. Pleasant, to have her so close, to have the arm and shoulder rubbed to warmth in that way. Must have learned the trick of it rubbing at her grandfather's aches and pains. Old rheumatics . . .

He stretched out under the buffalo robe, easing under the girl's thin, strong hands. Rubbing, stroking, pressing the stiffness away, drawing out the ache of it.

"You're a good girl," Lee said. "I told you not to shoot at that damn bear and you didn't do it.

"Good girl."

He turned on his back in the warmth of the buffalo robes, and the girl slid a skinny leg across his belly, and sat half up the better to lean her weight onto his arm and shoulder. She had strong hands for such a slight girl. Warmer now, too. Her skin was warm from the shelter of the robe, from the heat of their bodies together.

She dug her thumbs into the joint of Lee's shoulder where the pain, the stiffness seemed to be set, and seemed to search the discomfort out. Hurt as much as the ache itself at first, then slowly made it better.

Big nose or not, Lee was becoming mighty fond. *Charity* . . . in no way misnamed.

She shifted, stroking Lee's bruised shoulder, his arm, more lightly. Lee began to consider that the Cree Indians had a value considerably above other Redskins, if this sort of Swedish rubbing was a habit among them. Never heard that the Sioux or Comanche did such—the Blackfeet either. It seemed a greater gift than the artful scalping of white land agents and troopers had proved to be for those southern tribes.

"I want to thank you for this," Lee said, and surely meant it. He could clench his left hand now and feel only a shadow of pain up through his shoulder. Much better. The grizzly had clubbed him as a great baseball player might have done wielding a bat of stone. Felt a lot better. And here was Lee Morgan, sport and horse-rancher (and try not to think of chores left uncompleted on the Bit. Try not to think of the Mexican fever, the hoof-and-mouth. Not that far north, please God!) "Thank you," Lee said into the dark to an invisible girl, tall and scrawny, naked and mirror-smooth, boney as a bunch of sticks. Her shaggy, rough-cut hair smelled like a fox's pelt; her body smelled, too—a sharp, rich, animal smell. Dirt and sweat, campfire smoke. Slightly, the creamy scent of girl . . . the faint fish-stink of her privates.

Comforting . . . No saying it wasn't.

"That was pleasing . . . Charity."

No answer from the Indian girl. Silence from the Big-nose Cree.

Lee felt her thin leg shift against him . . . thought he could hear her breathing, just barely, above the soft sea-sounds of the wind through the hemlocks overhead. The wind through those tree tops sounded as it had sounded years before, off Seal Rock. Almost the same soft, heavy, insistent whispering.

"That was pleasing . . ."

He felt her shift her slight weight, start to

draw away from him under the robe. Lee reached up and took hold of her thin arm to hold her still—did it with his left hand, too. He slid his other hand up under the buffalo hide, found her skinny, smooth-skinned thigh (his hand reached halfway 'round it, she was so meager) and held it.

Charity made no further move to try and draw away; she stayed, half over, half beside him and was quiet under the shelter of the robe. Still beside him in that close and narrow place of warmth, so fragile in the circling leagues of forest, the freezing night.

Lee felt his cock stir, slowly rise against her narrow flank.

She was young—damn young. An Indian, though . . . had likely grunted under some drunken buck well before now. Must have, to come sashaying stark naked over to a man's bed roll. Young, though, and may have meant only to ease the aches . . .

She was quiet under his hands as a young rabbit might have been, frozen in terror, lifted by its nape from a trap. Lee likely should take his hands from her, let her go, let her walk back to her buffalo robe.

Surely should do that.

He caressed her thigh, stroking it gently, sliding his hand up along that smooth length slowly up to her ass. The Indian girl had hardly any ass at all—her little rounds of butt were almost as flat and muscular as a boy's. Lee fitted his hand to her small ass-cheek. It filled his hand nicely as if it had been made for just that purpose. He gripped and squeezed it, squeezed it hard enough to make her murmur in the darkness. She moved slightly so the skin of her hip rubbed smoothly against the heat and swelling of his cock.

Lee let go of her arm, put his hand to her throat, and slid it down her thin, tendon-corded neck to her chest, again, near flat as a boy's except where the small, surprising breasts grew like soft lemons with harder tips. She made to pull away when Lee touched her there, when he began to squeeze one of her breasts, took the nipple between his thumb and forefinger and pinched it lightly. Then barely touched it, his fingertip tapping it, brushing it . . . feeling, after a while, the small nipple fatten under his moving finger.

He began to tickle at her with his other hand, cupping the round of her ass that he had squeezed to hurting before and tracing the glossy smoothness of her skin there with his fingers. He slowly curled his fingers under her buttock cheek . . . felt the soft little button of her asshole . . . stroked it gently . . .

Lee felt the girl relax in his hands. It was a slight and subtle thing, a sagging into him . . . letting him bear her weight.

He reached further up under her, his fingers searching from her ass along the slight, downy rise of her cunt . . . found the tight, narrow little slot, and gently touched it, searched along it with his fingertips. Found a small damp place. Pushed harder with his finger.

The girl said something to him, twisted in his arms, but Lee held her hard, got his finger up into her, and pushed it deeper.

Felt something there. Something. Knew what it was, and didn't stop.

Lee rolled the girl over and under him, felt the night's hard cold fall across his shoulders where the robe slid away. The Cree girl clutched at him, strong, skinny fingers biting into the muscle of his arms, his shoulders. Lee's left arm ached as he leaned on it above her. He wished he could see her face, her eyes.

He bent over her, and, something to his own surprise, kissed her on the lips. Charity must not have done much white-style kissing; he felt her start when he kissed her, touched her half-parted lips with his tongue.

She tasted rich. Soft and sweet and rich.

Lee, braced over her, bent his head again and began to lick slowly along the thin plains of her face, her lips, her closed eyelids. He kissed the proud little beak of her nose, licked gently at her lips again, nuzzled her head to one side so that he could trace the delicate whorls of her ear with his tongue tip.

No question the missionary Cree was getting a lesson in the white man's mouth ways . . .

. . . And liking it.

Lee heard her sigh, felt her turn slightly beneath him as he kissed and sucked at her throat. It was startling, how good she tasted. Apparently it was the best sort of flavoring for a young girl, to have ridden high country for two or three days sweating or chilled, weary and unbathed. Gave this big-nosed little girl a fine high flavor . . .

Lee used his tongue along the lines of her slender throat, kissed her softly under the angle of her jaw. She had turned her small head in the dark, to present that place to him. *"The Colonel's lady, and Rosie O'Grady . . ."*

Lee found one of her breasts with his mouth, tongued the nipple, then sucked strongly on it. That pleased the girl very much, pleased her so that she cried out something in Indian. Then he pleased her at her other little breast and bit that nipple lightly, tugging at it.

He felt one of her hands then drifting slowly down between them. Slowly . . . slowly. Then her fingers found him. Lee would have known even if he hadn't already felt the evidence of it, that she was virgin. Would have known by the delicate, searching way she touched it, traced the swollen size of his cock, then lightly gripped it.

Her other hand slid down, and she held

him and gently squeezed at it, as if to test its hardness, its heat.

Lee had intended to lick her from armpits to toes, and all dark, sweet stops in between, but that gentle, faintly trembling grip changed his mind.

He crowded her under the buffalo robe, reached down to tug her knees apart, reached down between them when she spread them wide, obedient as a child. Touched her, found that small in-folded spot, wetter now under his fingertips. Slippery.

The Cree girl panted under him; her grip on his cock was not so gentle now. Her breathing was harsh as a dog's—Lee felt the touch of it on his cheeks. She was holding his cock, rubbing it, the tip of it, against her cunt. He felt the smooth heat against his, heard the faint sticky sound as she used him. Had done the like before, no doubt, used something long and hard to play with in that fashion . . .

She murmured something in the dark, pulled at him, thrust up just a little.

Time—and past time.

Lee sat back, reached down to her narrow hips to lift them up, then with one hand brushed her tentative hands away, gripped his cock, set it to the soft fork of her crotch, searched with it for that little oily place . . .

He found it, put the head of his cock hard against it. And pushed.

She grunted then tried to twist away, but Lee had her and meant to keep her. He thrust again—felt that veil of tissue snagging at his cock-head—and thrust into her with all his strength.

Charity screamed one short, sharp cry, then was silent, struggling. She kicked out, trying to escape the pain, her skinny legs tangled in the buffalo robe. Silent wrestling— Lee was careful to hold his head up, away from a bite. Set his hands to her hips and held her down with all his weight.

He gritted his teeth against the squeezing pressure of her narrow passage (hurt him a little, tell the truth) then thrust again, hard as he could. Fiery hot for all the cold night against his uncovered back, and didn't, for that moment, care if he killed her.

His cock drove into her like a great greased pole, opening her up, spreading her, shoving up inside her. It drove up into her all the way and she screamed again, and twisted on it as if it was killing her, as if it had entered the chambers of her heart.

Once there, Lee rested, lying on her, bearing her down with his weight, feeling the wonderful sensations of it—of being at once inside her, and in a way, within a new country, too. Her screams, her weeping— she was sobbing under him as any white girl might—meant very little to him.

Nothing but that entrance into her living guts meant much to Lee immediately.

It seemed a long time he lay with the thin Indian girl in their robe in the dark. Lay on her, and in her, and was very well pleased. She wept for a while, quieter and quieter, and Lee bent to kiss her, kiss the tears.

He was still buried deep inside her, and hard as any stone.

It was still a while after that before he slowly began to move, over her murmured protests, her fluttering, staying hands. He moved slowly, slowly, deeper and then almost out of her, and took great care in doing it.

It took a long time before, still crying out softly at the pain now and again, the Big-nose girl commenced to dance with him the oldest dance of all.

Until, gasping, her small cunt and ass soaked with her juices, trembling as she received the long, pumping stokes, Big-nose Charity, grandaughter of Stones-Made-Shiny-By-Water, threw back her head in the cold night dark, kicked out in desperation at her pleasure, and screamed with delight.

Lee groaned and filled her—spurted his heart right out into her, so that the jissom leaked in blurts where they joined. It was so sweet, it made him shake, gasp for breath . . .

He loved her, then, for the while. Loved everything about her. "Sweetheart . . ." he called her then, and the girl heard him.

Lee woke late, after dawn, to a dark and

windy morning. There was the barest tracery of snow laced across the forest floor—damned if he knew when it had fallen. Touches of it still decorated the spreading fronds of the hemlocks overhead.

Must have slept like an Irishman on a work day to have missed the fall of snow.

Lee rolled over in the buffalo robe, and saw Charity at the morning fire, setting the coffee pot on. She worked with her head lowered, not looking at him. Ashamed, likely, of what they'd done last night. Could thank the missionaries for that. Roman Catholics as bad as the Protestants. Same superstitious nonsense.

"Good morning . . ."

She glanced up, murmured a "Good morning" back, then went on with her work, feeding the fire more fallen wood, working it up despite the wind that gusted through the camp. She did it well—that would be a good cooking fire.

Hadn't noticed the snow—hadn't wakened to it. Hadn't felt the girl getting up, either. Seemed that a scramble with a bear made for deep sleeping.

Lee lay back, stretching, trying his left shoulder, the sore arm. Better. Both were better. The rubbing—and the other—had eased the hurt considerably. Cold day, cold enough to snow again, more heavily. He wouldn't miss that one. Wind was hissing through these trees like snakes, fluttering the fire.

Time to roll out and get doing, and Lee started to do just that.

"I believe that I could pink this Yankee nicely through the skull—would you say so, Robins?"

"I would indeed, m'Lord. Sittin'—or in flight."

Lee held still—made no move at all. They had come up into the wind, likely smelling camp smoke all the way. Must have canoed down the river to the mountain's base, quartered the forest, and waited for Lee to make a mistake. Something foolish, like building fires in strange country just so as to be warm and have a hot breakfast.

Lee looked across at Charity and saw she was startled. Not from her, then, nor with her. Poor little Dowd must have cried out too particularly as he lay dying.

They'd expected him.

CHAPTER NINE

Very slowly, Lee turned to see the men. He was up on one elbow, still half in the buffalo robe, and naked. The Bisley Colt's was an arms-reach away to the side, holstered, resting neatly on folds of cartridge belt, protected from the snow by a flap of slicker.

Just an arm's reach away—and distant from use as a shotgun in Brady's hardware in Parker, Idaho.

The English boy was beautiful even in his furs and gaiters. Looked like a fine blonde woman, a tall and merry one, but for a fair breadth of shoulder and the size of his hands. He held a heavy Webley revolver in his right hand, and the revolver was not too big for his grip.

"Good morning to you, Mister . . . ?" The boy had bright blue eyes; his silver hair curled like fine sheep's wool. His voice was pitched so high, so musically, that it sounded like singing.

He seemed to be a proper English lord, Lee thought. Proper enough to have played one on the stage.

"Morgan," Lee said. "Lee Morgan."

The beautiful boy nodded and strolled over to the fire. He kept his eyes, and the muzzle of the big Webley, directed where Lee lay like a cadet surprised in bed with the sheriff's wife. Caught like a jackass, and like to be dealt with accordingly. Lee had no doubts the boy intended to kill him, though he appeared to enjoy taking his time about it, and hunkered by the fire like an old mossy horn, warming his elegant bottom by the fire's heat, facing Lee, watching him, smiling. He was only a little farther from the holstered Colt's then Lee was, and Lee knew that the boy knew all the thoughts being thought about that weapon.

"I shouldn't if I were you," Lord Surrey said, indicating the Colt's with a raised eyebrow. "Simply too far from you, dear fellow. Too far."

Couldn't argue with the sissy son-of-a-bitch on that.

"You—girl." Surrey turned his head just a little toward her. "If that's coffee—and I suppose it must be, despite its odor—you may pour me a cup, and bring it to me."

Charity kept her eyes lowered, as though she didn't want to see any of them, as though she didn't want to see anything at all.

She picked the pot up out of the coals, poured a measure into a tin cup, and came around the fire at a slow half-crouch, looking scared to death.

Lee didn't blame her. But he didn't feel afraid, himself. Felt angry at dying a fool's death but did not feel afraid.

He looked slowly 'round again and saw "Robins." The Earl's man was a small, neat, well-set-up fellow, with a pale, pinched face. Looked like a game keeper, by his stance, the easy way he cradled a double-barrelled shotgun. He appeared to know how to use a shotgun. He seemed very easy with it.

Lee saw no way. There was a chance, of course, that he might get to the Bisley and take only one round from the smiling boy's revolver in doing it. Might be fit then, to draw and shoot the holstered Colt's—or might not. There was a chance of his doing that, though more than likely Surrey would have put two or more rounds into him. More than likely would have blown his fool head off, as it deserved.

Still there was a *slight* chance of using the Colt's. Except for Robins. Surrey's man would certainly not miss with that shotgun at this range even if his master did.

Charity handed the pretty boy his coffee,

serving carefully, and from her decorous crouch, a servant born, a savage well tamed and trained.

The boy sipped his coffee and regarded Lee. He seemed amused. "It was, I believe, a social solecism to have come upon you in such a . . . state of nature, my dear fellow." He sipped again. "Your friend, the minute Mister Dowd, though greedy and a trespasser, had at least the fortune of facing us in his night-shirt. An extraordinary sight he was, too. That shirt, Robins—was it yellow-striped, or puce?"

The servant's voice came back over Lee's shoulder. "Puce, m'lord." That voice, fat with satisfaction at its subordination to this murdering rich pup, made Lee's skin crawl. To be done by such a pair as this, and all his own fault! His own fault . . . lying out in soogins like a drunken Paddy . . . toasting himself at a damned bonfire . . .

Close to, the earl wasn't quite as beautiful a boy as he'd seemed. Had a trace too much jaw . . . a length too much nose to match it.

"To go to one's Maker in such a state," the young lord said, "is to compound one's stupidity in going at all, in such a cause." He'd stopped smiling. "The theft of another man's land is the one unforgivable crime." Boy sounded as if he meant it. The smile was as distant as the season of Spring, now. Lord Surrey looked like a hangman, one of the fortunate that enjoyed that work. "You," the handsome boy added, and took a third sip of coffee, "I consider to be an aider and abettor of Mister Dowd's attempted theft." He'd had enough coffee now or simply wished both hands free and handed the cup to Charity to take away. "And I intend to deal with you as appropriately . . ." Charity went crouching away behind him to the fire, the cup held as if the boy's lips had plated it with gold.

The Webley came level.

It seemed to Lee that it was a very large-bored weapon. Forty-five caliber or over, it looked to him . . . Lee took a deep breath.

"Head-shot, Robins?"

"Oh, I should think so, m'lord, at that range . . ."

Lee saw Charity, obscured behind the boy, slowly stand up, appear to draw back both her hands. Then, as if she were swinging a baseball bat, in a swift, hard sideways motion, she stepped closer to Lord Surrey and hit him hard in the back.

"What the devil did you *do?!*" The boy stood straight up, his voice going high as a girl's, astonished. He turned 'round on her, one hand a fist to strike her down—and Lee saw the hunting knife handle, the blade sunk deep beside his spine.

Lee rolled for the holstered Colt's and took that infernal buffalo robe with him, tangled at his legs.

The movement of turning must have stirred the steel and sliced inside what shouldn't be cut, for the boy who must have felt at first only the thump of impact as she struck him, suddenly strained up on his toes —up and then arching back so far that Lee thought his back must break from the posture.

"Oh!" the boy shouted. "Oh, dear—oh, *dear!*" He spun on his toes like a dancer, the knife hilt sticking like a long peg from his back, then fell face first into the fire.

Lee had the buffalo robe kicked free, had the Bisley out and cocked and saw Charity, her narrow beaky face well pleased, suddenly struck in the throat by a shotgun charge. Blood blew from her slight neck in a furious spray, and Lee rolled to his belly, half turned to fire over his left shoulder, and placed his first round into the servant's groin.

Even shot so and hard hit, Robins reshouldered the shotgun and swung it smooth as a safe door down at Lee, the pinched, pale face as set as bread pudding.

Lee shot him again, through the stomach, and in spasm, the man pulled his second trigger. The buckshot hissed across the clearing and rattled into a tree, and Lee fired at the son-of-a-bitch a third time (hasty and despairing, Charity on his mind) aimed poorly and shot the falling man's lower jaw away, leaving a bright white splinter under the servant's sprouting tongue as he fell stretched out beneath a great green fan of hemlock branches.

Lee got to his feet naked in the freezing air, which he felt not at all, and saw Charity dying on the other side of the fire where the young lord crawled and muttered, his fine hair burning, his face frying, combing the seething coals.

When Lee reached her she was all but bled completely out, lying on her back, her thin, dark hands held half above her as if to ward off some terrible descending blow. Her hands, her whole slight body was slowly clenching into spasm, then relaxing, after. Her slender neck was hacked wide open, torn away by the shotgun charge. She was so drenched in blood she looked made of bronze —a statue memorial of a dying Indian girl.

She smelled of salt from all the blood when Lee took her in his arms—a dead girl, near as might be.

"I love you," the horse-rancher said, and meant it. She might have heard it, but likely not.

It took Lee more time than he'd thought to put her away.

He'd dressed himself, put her fine beaver parka on her, then wrapped her in the robe they'd shared, corded that around her, tight and then, burdened by her, had carefully climbed up through the thick low branches of the largest hemlock over the camp, to lash her high in the air, safe near the trunk of the tree.

Then he'd gone into the forest a way to find the hobbled horses, and brought them into camp (they'd shied at the stink of the handsome young Earl who, still and silent at last, crouched in the bed of dying fire, his roasted buttocks in the air, his face an eyeless char, Charity's knife still stuck in his back.

Lee tacked the animals out, and struck camp.

He had ridden less than a mile, perhaps a good deal less in this forest, (umbrella'd by such trees, distance was a chancy thing to tell) when he heard a man laughing behind him.

It was a faint sound and a good distance back, but it was laughter right enough, and a kind to set a chill down Lee's back. Nothing mad or loony about it—no inhumanity.

Simply the free and open laughter of a man who'd come upon something very funny.

A fellow with his jaw shot off, say. And a well-cooked Earl.

Lee wondered if the Frenchman would try a slice of Surrey, so providentially prepared. Wondered, too, why the trapper had not been with the others when they took the camp. Forge had loitered for some reason—perhaps weary of the young Lord's company, peerhaps the other way 'round, and the Englishmen had found the cannibal's company unsettling—and so had arrived too late for that fight. Lee had no illusions that he

196

might have survived if the Frenchman had joined the others earlier.

He was only alive now because the Indian girl had felt a duty to him—out of love, perhaps, or out of gratitude for the pleasures he had shared with her the night before, or, and most likely, out of duty as his guide. She, a meager girl, had not failed where her grandfather had failed.

Lee did not care to think where he had failed in his duty to her. He built a wall of seasoned timber in his mind against those thoughts and rode the tall grey and led the sturdy, ambling paint down dark aisles of forest, slowly circling back toward that distant, merry sound of laughter.

Poor chance, of course, against such a woodsman in such a wood, but a chance to be taken just the same. This was the last fellow Lee had come to see, and there was no riding south without.

Did not care to think . . .

The Frenchman, after all, would not be killing much, should he do Lee down. Dowd at least had brought a gunman with him into danger when he went hunting land and grants and leases.

Lee had brought a big-nosed girl, fifteen years old, perhaps. Maybe sixteen . . .

The Frenchman, if he was lucky enough, and clever, would be killing a fellow looked like a man, was tall, and strong. Was fierce and quick with weapons. Looked like a man, sure enough, but rang hollow in the clinch. Had, in the past, brought home death to his father. Had now brought another here to death.

Sill, even such a person as that will "try the last."

Lee dug spurs to the grey and that fine horse went galloping. They threaded at speed through stands of rough-barked trunks, the grey dashing past in quick curves or in between so close and so fast that Lee's stirrup irons struck the trees at times to one side or the other as he leaned with the horse on the turns. The paint pounded after.

No use trying to sneak a march on a master trapper. The Frenchman would duck and dodge, hide and conceal and laugh that ringing merry laugh of his as Lee came stumbling after, clumsy on horseback.

Only chance was to rush him—to come in fast and at a run, to hasty the man (or anger him) into a present fight. Lee bent low over the saddle-bow as the grey drove headlong into a rare clump of brush—bulled and battered through, and ran reaching out the other side. Branches were striking like spade handles at Lee as he galloped past. His Stetson went at one, and a second and third branch hit out at him and almost clubbed him from the saddle. There was no bending low enough in that tangle at a run to keep from being scraped and lashed at, keep from being beaten.

He was almost back at camp—was sure he was almost at it, when the grey was shot at and hit and killed all in a single stride.

Lee never heard the shot—wouldn't have above the horses' slamming hooves that shook even this soft forest floor, the crash and crackle of the greenery as they went galloping through. Never heard the shot, but felt the grey falter as the jolt went through it —felt the animal's legs fold beneath it like a duck's wing as it is shot—felt the grey pitching headlong into its fall.

Lee unstirruped, rolled out of his saddle to the right, struck soft ground and not, by good luck, a tree, and was up and running, Bisley Colt's in his hand, toward the camp now no more than some yards away, and the place for sure where a rifle round must have started, to have caught the grey so neatly at his right shoulder. Lee'd felt that jolt in his right leg as it lay along the grey's barrel.

Lee ran through the last of the low hemlock branches and got a smart cut along his left cheek-bone doing it, then charged into the camp clearing (matters now seeming to move slowly, as if in a dream, as if he had time and enough to spare for any action).

The clearing was empty.

Silence.

No bird sounds. The sun, in this almost

open spot, came dappling down in small splashes on the dark pine straw underfoot.

No sign of the Frenchman at all—not even the faintest smell of gun-powder, either. Or haze of it.

Lee heard the paint, deprived of its customary companion and trail lead, blundering about in the woods beyond.

Otherwise, silence.

Lee stood in the camp's center, armed. Where he looked, the muzzle of the Bisley Colt's turned also, a bright, vacant, inquiring eye. Forge had not taken his opportunity of cooked meat. Neither dead man had been disturbed, only laughed at. Lee wondered if the Frenchman was a big man; he surely was a swift one.

Perhaps had had some fun or other with the girl's body. Signs of climbing and scrape and fuss would have led Forge there as surely as a street sign would a city clerk.

Lee, stopping once to watch behind him, stepped over to that hemlock, under it, and peered up into the branches.

He saw the darker shape of the girl's wrapped corpse, undisturbed.

And beside it, crouching, smiling down at him, a bulky man with a rosy, merry face, clean-shaven as a Catholic monk. The man, in the instant Lee had to look, was dressed in a fringed fur coat and had upon his head a round fur hat with a sprig of green tucked into it.

The Frenchman dropped down onto Lee like a stooping hawk, and as he fell, brought down a bright-bladed hatchet as Lee brought his revolver up, and struck the Colt's clean out of Lee's hand as the man himself struck Lee and drove him to the ground.

They rolled there for an instant, Lee managing by great luck to grip the trapper's hatchet-arm at the wrist. It was luck, and only of the moment, because the Frenchman was sickeningly strong. Now Lee knew the man was mad, no matter how healthy his laughter. Forge was too strong not to be mad.

Lee could do that range-country strong man's trick of bending horse shoes . . . could loop an iron poker, too. And had won bets more than once, arm or Indian wrestling iron-muscled drovers and wranglers and teamsters. Was, in fact, reckoned a dangerously strong man and of course, wonderfully quick. Little use, now.

Forge rolled with Lee on the pine needle carpet, beaming with apparent great pleasure all the while, pulled his wrist from Lee's grip with no seeming effort at all and struck with the hatchet again.

The edge of the blade sliced a small piece of Lee's cheek away—about as much as could have been covered by a silver dollar—and then buried itself in the forest floor.

Forge had it out and struck again as Lee threw himself back and away. The blade caught him lightly across his left forearm, and Lee felt and heard the faint *snick* as it nicked the bone there. Lee leaped up and backward for his life. Forge, still pleasant in the face, came up and after him faster than a man should have been able and Lee stepped back into the charred dead branches of the fire, tripped, tripped again as he tried to balance, and fell full back into the crouched corpse of the English boy.

The Frenchman chuckled, or made that sort of sound, and drove across the ashes to seize Lee and butcher him just as he rolled clear of the toppled corpse.

The Frenchman drove down, seized Lee by his hair, hauled him up to his knees, and held him close. The hatchet went swinging up and back.

Lee stabbed the Frenchman in the balls with Charity's hunting knife, wrenched it out, and stabbed the man again.

The hatchet's bright blade hung still in the air, as if Forge had been turned to stone. Stabbing a third time, driving the long blade deep, deep up into the trapper's privates, up into his bowels, Lee still felt that dreadful grip clenched upon his hair, still saw, high over the Frenchman's head, his raised arm, the gleaming hatchet head.

The cannibal stood seeming frozen as stone, either by the mortal wounds, or the agony of them, or by the sudden knowledge of death present.

The man stood stock still in that fashion—

his fist still clenched in Lee's hair, the hatchet raised—for several seconds. Then as Lee worked and worked the killing blade inside him, Farge lowered his hatchet arm, as if reluctantly, slowly crouched, and began to grunt in an odd, rhythmic way, as if he were moving his bowels. Then he let go Lee's hair, squatted down, and rolled over onto his side.

The man was muscled like a run-wild hog, and Lee had much ado to carve his lower belly open as he kicked, reach in, and stab him to the heart.

Took a good while to stanch the bleeding from Lee's sliced cheek. His left forearm hardly bled at all, but was badly swollen and colored purple where the cannibal's blade had clicked on bone. Lee thought that he might lose that arm . . .

Still, he did his musts. He stanched his cheek and cleaned and bound his chopped forearm as best he could. He found the Colt's and holstered it. He walked out into the woods to find the wandering paint, to take what he needed from the body of the grey.

The day had turned to noon by the time he'd finished all this. Bright noon, and very cold, as he mounted the paint to ride.

There would be snow before night, and he, lonely as the far side of the moon, would ride solitary through a forest white as death.

MAKE SURE YOU HAVE ALL THE BOOKS IN LEISURE'S RED-HOT *BUCKSKIN* SERIES

IF YOU ENJOYED BUCKSKIN'S ADVENTURES, BE SURE TO ORDER LEISURE'S HOT-AS-A-PISTOL *SPUR* SERIES

BLAZING WESTERN ADVENTURE BY *SPUR* AWARD WINNER NELSON NYE

2108-0	**A LOST MINE NAMED SALVATION**	$2.25
2150-1	**BORN TO TROUBLE**	$2.25
2214-1	**QUICK-TRIGGER COUNTRY**	$2.25
2253-2	**CARTRIDGE CASE LAW**	$2.25
2295-8	**THE OVERLANDERS**	$2.25

MORE HARD-RIDING, STRAIGHT-SHOOTING WESTERN ADVENTURE FROM LEISURE BOOKS

Make the Most of Your Leisure Time with
LEISURE BOOKS

Please send me the following titles:

Quantity	Book Number	Price
_____	_____	_____
_____	_____	_____
_____	_____	_____
_____	_____	_____

If out of stock on any of the above titles, please send me the alternate title(s) listed below:

_____	_____	_____
_____	_____	_____
_____	_____	_____
_____	_____	_____

	Postage & Handling	_____
	Total Enclosed	$ _____

☐ Please send me a free catalog.

NAME _____
(please print)

ADDRESS _____

CITY _____ STATE _____ ZIP _____

Please include $1.00 shipping and handling for the first book ordered and 25¢ for each book thereafter in the same order. All orders are shipped within approximately 4 weeks via postal service book rate. PAYMENT MUST ACCOMPANY ALL ORDERS.*

*Canadian orders must be paid in US dollars payable through a New York banking facility.

Mail coupon to: **Dorchester Publishing Co., Inc.**
6 East 39 Street, Suite 900
New York, NY 10016
Att: ORDER DEPT.